Praise for VELOCITIES: STORIES

"A modern genius of weird and dark fiction, Kathe Ko[ja shows] with *Velocities* that she's adept at plunging the read[er into] unexpected places. One of my favorite collectio[ns...]"
—**Jeff Vandermeer, NYT-bestselling author of *Dead Astronauts*, *Borne* and the Southern Reach trilogy**

"*Velocities* is prime Kathe Koja, with all that that entails: supercharged, dense as hell, oblique, glorious. Every story is a lesson in how to write faster, more intensely, from angles other people never seem to think of: industrial poetry, word mosaics like insect eyes, multifoliate as the insides of flowers, every image a scattered, burrowing seed, spreading narrative like a disease. I've loved her work since long before I ever aspired to produce anything like it—in fact, I'm still not sure anyone else is capable of doing what she does, of coming close, let alone hitting the mark. But damn, it's equally so much fun to admire the result as it is to even vaguely try."
—**Gemma Files, award-winning author of *Spectral Evidence***

"Velocities is immersive, hypnotic, yet clear-eyed and accessible. These are dangerous, artful tales of mounting tension, impossible to put down. Koja's fiction has never seemed more alive or daring."
—**Douglas Clegg, award-winning author of *Neverland* and *The Faces***

"Short sharp speedballs of strange. Incantatory, funny, human—ranging from urban dread, to country nightmares, to bite-sized fables so baroque and twisted, you can taste the corruption on your tongue and in your dreams."
—**J.S. Breukelaar, author of *Collision: Stories* and *Aletheia***

"An impressive collection of stories unafraid to explore bleak topics like death and despondency."
—***Kirkus Reviews***

"Reading Velocities is a literary dégustation of dark fiction with speculative elements, rich narrative full of text that's cunning, loaded with sentiment. . . . Read Koja like you're nibbling truffles, each bite a road to metamorphosis."
—**Eugen Bacon, *Aurealis Magazine***

VELO/ CITIES

S T O R I E S

KATHE KOJA

Meerkat Press
Atlanta

"At Eventide," originally published in *Graven Images: Fifteen Tales of Magic and Myth*, edited by Nancy Kilpatrick and Thomas S. Roche, Penguin Ace, 2000
"Baby," originally published in *Teeth: Vampire Tales*, edited by Ellen Datlow and Terri Windling, HarperCollins, 2011
"Velocity," originally published in *The Dark: New Ghost Stories*, edited by Ellen Datlow, Tor Books, 2004
"Clubs," originally published in *Witness*, Volume IX, No. 1, 1995
"Urb Civ," originally published in *Nowheresville*, edited by Scott Gable and C. Dombrowski, Broken Eye Books, 2019
"Fireflies," originally published in *Asimov's Science Fiction*, 2006
"Road Trip," originally published in *World Fantasy Convention Guest of Honor Program Book* and in *The Year's Best Fantasy and Horror 16*, edited by Ellen Datlow and Terri Windling, St. Martin's Griffin, 2002
"Toujours," originally published in *Blood and Other Cravings*, edited by Ellen Datlow, Tor Books, 2011
"Far and Wee," originally published in *Werewolves and Shapeshifters: Encounters with the Beast Within*, edited by John Skipp, Black Dog & Leventhal, 2010.
"La Reine d'Enfer," originally published in *Queen Victoria's Book of Spells*, edited by Ellen Datlow and Terri Windling, Tor Books, 2013
"Pas de Deux," originally published in *Dark Love*, edited by Nancy A. Collins, Edward E. Kramer and Martin H. Greenberg, ROC Books, 1995

Author Photo by Rick Lieder
Cover and book design by Tricia Reeks

ISBN-13 978-1-946154-23-1 (Paperback)
ISBN-13 978-1-946154-24-8 (eBook)

Library of Congress Control Number: 2020933245

Printed in the United States of America

Published in the United States of America by
Meerkat Press, LLC, Atlanta, Georgia
www.meerkatpress.com

Thanks to Tricia Reeks for the smooth ride,
and as ever to Christopher Schelling

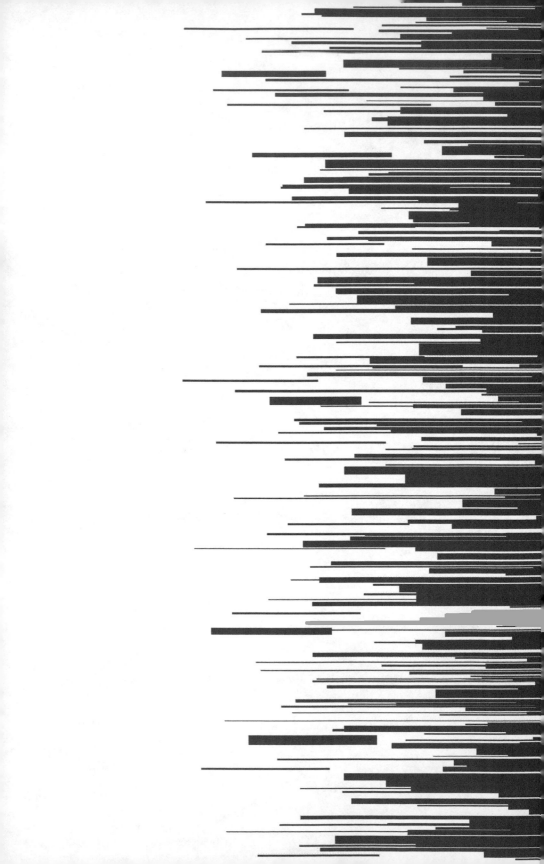

AT HOME

DOWNTOWN

ON THE WAY

OVER THERE

INSIDE

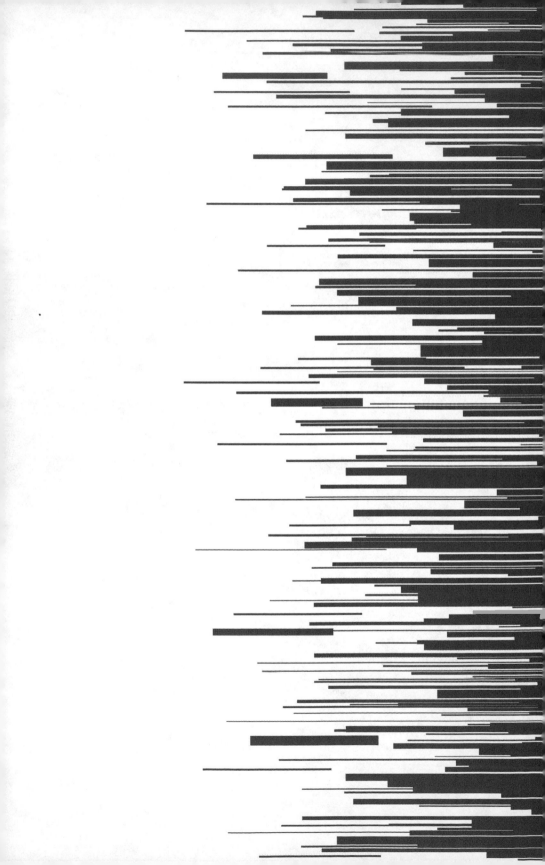

AT HOME

AT EVENTIDE

What he carried to her he carried in a red string bag. Through its mesh could be seen the gleam and tangle of new wire, a package of wood screws, a green plastic soda bottle, a braided brown coil of human hair; a wig? It could have been a wig.

To get to her he had come a long way: from a very large city through smaller cities to Eventide, not a city at all or even a town, just the nearest outpost of video store and supermarket, gas and ice and cigarettes. The man at the Stop-N-Go had directions to her place, a map he had sketched himself; he spoke as if he had been there many times: "It's just a little place really, just a couple rooms, living room and a workshop; there used to be a garage out back but she had it knocked down."

The man pointed at the handmade map; there was something wrong with his voice, cancer maybe, a sound like bones in the throat; he did not look healthy. "It's just this feeder road, all the way down?"

"That's right. Takes about an hour, hour and ten, you can be there before dark if you—"

"Do you have a phone?"

"Oh, I don't have her number. And anyway you don't call first, you just drive on down there and—"

"A phone," the man said; he had not changed his tone, he had not raised his voice, but the woman sorting stock at the back of the store half-rose, gripping like a brick a cigarette carton.

The man behind the counter lost his smile, and "Right over there," he said, pointing past the magazine rack bright with tabloids, with PLAYBOY and NASTY GIRLS and JUGGS; he lit a cigarette while the man made his phone call, checked with a wavering glance the old Remington 870 beneath the counter.

But the man finished his call, paid for his bottled water and sunglasses, and left in a late model pickup, sober blue, a rental probably, and "I thought," said the woman with the cigarette cartons, "that he was going to try something."

"So did I," said the man behind the counter. The glass doors opened to let in heat and light, a little boy and his tired mother, a tropical punch Slush Puppie and a loaf of Wonder bread.

• • •

Alison, the man said into the phone. It's me.

A pause: no sound at all, no breath, no sigh; he might have been talking to the desert itself. Then: Where are you? she said. What do you want?

I want one of those boxes, he said. The ones you make. I'll bring you everything you need.

Don't come out here, she said, but without rancor; he could imagine her face, its Goya coloring, the place where her eye had been. Don't bring me anything, I can't do anything for you.

See you in an hour, the man said. An hour and ten.

• • •

He drove the feeder road to the sounds of Mozart, '40s show tunes, flashy Tex-Mex pop; he drank bottled water; his throat hurt from the air conditioning, a flayed unchanging ache. Beside him sat the string bag, bulging loose and uneven, like a body with a tumor, many tumors; like strange fruit; like a bag of gold from a fairy tale. The hair in the bag was beautiful, a thick and living bronze like the pelt of an animal, a thoroughbred, a beast prized for its fur. He had braided it carefully, with skill and a certain love, and secured it at the bottom with a small blue plastic bow. The other items in the bag he had purchased at a hardware store, just like he used to; the soda bottle he had gotten at the airport, and emptied in the men's room sink.

There was not much scenery, unless you like the desert, its lunar space, its brutal endlessness; the man did not. He was a creature of cities, of pocket parks and dull anonymous bars; of waiting rooms and holding cells; of emergency clinics; of pain. In the beige plastic box beneath the truck's front seat there were no less than eight different pain medications, some in liquid form, some in pills, some in patches; on his right bicep, now, was the vague itch of a Fentanyl patch. The doctor had warned him about driving while wearing it: *There might be some confusion,* the doctor said, *along with the sedative effect. Maybe a headache, too.*

A headache, the man had repeated; he thought it was funny. *Don't worry, doctor. I'm not going anywhere.* Two hours later he was on a plane to New Mexico. Right now the Fentanyl was working, but only just; he had an assortment of patches in various amounts—25, 50, 100 milligrams—so he could mix and match them as needed, until he wouldn't need them anymore.

Now Glenn Gould played Bach, which was much better than Fentanyl. He turned down the air conditioning and turned the music up loud, dropping his hand to the bag on the seat, fingers worming slowly through the mesh to touch the hair.

• • •

They brought her what she needed, there in the workshop: they brought her her life. Plastic flowers, fraying T-shirts, rosaries made of shells and shiny gold; school pictures, wedding pictures, wedding rings, books; surprising how often there were books. Address books, diaries, romance novels, murder mysteries, Bibles; one man even brought a book he had written himself, a ruffled stack of printer paper tucked into a folding file.

Everything to do with the boxes she did herself: she bought the lumber, she had a lathe, a workbench, many kinds and colors of stain and varnish; it was important to her to do everything herself. The people did their part, by bringing the objects—the baby clothes and car keys, the whiskey bottles and Barbie dolls; the rest was up to her.

Afterward they cried, some of them, deep tears strange and bright in the desert, like water from the rock; some of them thanked her, some cursed her, some said nothing at all but took their boxes away: to burn them, pray to them, set them on a shelf for everyone to see, set them in a closet where no one could see. One woman had sold hers to an art gallery, which had started no end of problems for her, out there in the workshop, the problems imported by those who wanted to visit her, interview her, question her about the boxes and her methods, and motives, for making them. Totems, they called them, or Rorschach boxes, called her a shaman of art, a priestess, a doctor with a hammer and an "uncanny eye." They excavated her background, old pains exposed like bones; they trampled her silence, disrupted her work, and worst of all, they sicced the world on her, a world of the sad and the needy, the desperate, the furious and lost. In a very short time it became more than she could handle, more than anyone could handle, and she thought about leaving the country, about places past the border that no one could find but in the end settled for a period of hibernation, then moved to Eventide and points south, the older, smaller workshop, the bleached and decayed garage that a man with a bulldozer had kindly destroyed for her; she had made him a box about his granddaughter, a box he had cradled as if it were the child herself. He was a generous man, he wanted to do something to repay her although "no one," he said, petting the box, "could pay for this. There ain't no money in the world to pay for this."

She took no money for the boxes, for her work; she never had. Hardly anyone could understand that: the woman who had sold hers to the gallery had gotten a surprising price, but money was so far beside the *point, there was no point in even discussing it, if you had to ask, and so on. She had money enough to live on, the damages had bought the house, and besides, she was paid already, wasn't she?—paid by the doing, in the doing, paid by peace and silence and the certain knowledge of help. The boxes helped them, always: sometimes the help of comfort, sometimes the turning knife, but sometimes the knife was what they needed; she never judged, she only did the work.*

Right now she was working on a new box, a clean steel frame to enclose the life inside: her life: she was making a box for herself. Why? and why now? but she didn't ask that, why was the one question she never asked, not of the ones who came to her, not now of herself. It was enough to do it, to gather the items, let her hand choose between this one and that: a hair clip shaped like a feather, a tube of desert dirt, a grimy nail saved from the wrecked garage; a photo of her mother, her own name in newsprint, a hospital bracelet snipped neatly in two. A life was a mosaic, a picture made from scraps: her boxes were only pictures of that picture and whatever else they might be or become—totems, altars, fetish objets—they were lives first, a human arc in miniature, a precis of pain and wonder made of homely odds and ends.

Her head ached from the smell of varnish, from squinting in the sawdust flume, from the heat; she didn't notice. From the fragments on the table before her, the box was coming into life.

• • •

He thought about her as he drove. The Fentanyl seemed to relax him, stretch his memories like taffy, warm and ropy, pull at his brain without tearing it, as the pain so often did. Sometimes the pain made him do strange things: once he had tried to drink boiling water, once he had flung himself out of a moving cab. Once he woke blinking on a restaurant floor, something hard jammed in his mouth, an EMS tech above him: *'Bout swallowed his tongue,* the tech said to the restaurant manager, who stood watching with sweat on his face. *People think that's just a figure of speech, you know, but they wrong.*

He had been wrong himself, a time or two: about his own stamina, the state of his health; about *her*, certainly. He had thought she would die easily; she had not died at all. He had thought she could not see him, but even with one eye she picked him out of a lineup, identified him in the courtroom, that long finger pointing, accusing, dismissing, all in one gesture, wrist arched like a bullfighter's before he places the killing blade, like a dancer's *en pointe*, poised to force truth out of air and bone: with that finger she said who he was and everything he was not, *mene, mene, tekel, upharsin*. It was possible to admire such certainty.

And she spared herself nothing; he admired her for that, too. Every day in the courtroom, before the pictures the prosecutor displayed: terrible Polaroids, all gristle and ooze, police tape and matted hair, but she looked, she listened carefully to everything that was said, and when the foreman said *guilty,* she listened to that, too; by then the rest of her hair had come in, just dark brown down at first but it grew back as lush as before. Beautiful hair . . . it was what he had noticed first about her, in the bar, the Blue Monkey, filled with art school students and smoke, the smell of cheap lager; he had tried to buy her a drink but *No thanks*, she had said, and turned away. Not one of the students, one of his usual prey, she was there and not-there at the same time, just as she was in his workshop later, there to the wire and the scalping knife, not-there to the need in his eyes.

In the end he had gotten nothing from her; and he admired her for that, too.

When he saw the article in the magazine—pure chance, really, just a half-hour's numb distraction, *Bright Horizons,* in the doctor's office, one of the doctors, he could no longer tell them apart—he felt in his heart an unaccustomed emotion: gratitude. Cleaved from him as the others had been, relegated to the jail of memory, but there she was, alive and working in the desert, in a workshop filled with tools that—did she realize?—he himself might have used, working in silence and diligence on that which brought peace to herself and pure release to others; they were practically colleagues, though he knew she would have resisted the comparison, she was a good one for resisting. The one who got away.

He took the magazine home with him; the next day he bought a map of New Mexico and a new recording of Glenn Gould.

• • •

She would have been afraid if it were possible, but fear was not something she carried; it had been stripped from her, scalped from her, in that room with the stuttering overheads, the loud piano music and the wire. Once the worst has happened, you lose the place where the fear begins; what's left is only scar tissue, like old surgery, like the dead pink socket of her eye. She did not wait for him, check the roads anxiously for him, call the police on him; the police had done her precious little good last time, they were only good for cleaning up, and she could clean up on her own, now, here in the workshop, here where the light fell empty, hard and perfect, where she cut with her X-Acto knife a tiny scrolling segment from a brand-new Gideon Bible: blessed are the merciful, for they shall obtain mercy.

Her hand did not shake as she used the knife; the light made her brown hair glow.

• • •

The man at the Stop-N-Go gave good directions: already he could see the workshop building, the place where the garage had been. He wondered how many people had driven up this road as he did, heart high, carrying what they needed, what they wanted her to use; he wondered how many had been in pain as he was in pain; he wondered what she said to them, what she might say to him now. Again he felt that wash of gratitude, that odd embodied glee; then the pain stirred in him like a serpent, and he had to clench his teeth to hold the road.

When he pulled up beside her workshop, he paused in the dust his car had raised to peel off the used patch and apply a fresh one; a small one, one of the 25 milligrams. He did not want to be drowsy, or distracted; he did not want sedation to dilute what they would do.

• • •

He looked like her memories, the old bad dreams, yet he did not; in the end he could have been anyone, any aging tourist with false new sunglasses and a sick man's careful gait, come in hope and sorrow to her door; in his hand he held a red string bag, she could see some of what was inside. She stood in the doorway waiting, the X-Acto knife in her palm; she did not wish he would go away, or that he had not come, wishing was a vice she had abandoned long ago, and anyway the light here could burn any wish to powder, it was one of the desert's greatest gifts. The other one was solitude; and now they were alone.

• • •

"Alison," he said. "You're looking good."

She said nothing. A dry breeze took the dust his car had conjured; the air was clear again. She said nothing.

"I brought some things," he said, raising the bag so she could see: the wires, the bottle, the hair; her hair. "For the box, I mean . . . I read about it in a magazine, about you, I mean."

Those magazines: like a breadcrumb trail, would he have found her without one? wanted to find her, made the effort on his own? Like the past to the present, one step leading always to another, and the past rose in her now, another kind of cloud: she did not fight it but let it rise, knew it would settle again as the dust had settled; and it did. He was still watching her. He still had both his eyes, but other things were wrong with him, his voice for one, and the way he walked, as if stepping directly onto broken glass, and "You don't ask me," he said, "how I got out."

"I don't care," she said. "You can't do anything to me."

"I don't want to. What I want," gesturing with the bag, his shadow reaching for her as he moved, "is for you to make a box for me. Like you do for other people. Make a box of my life, Alison."

No answer; she stood watching him as she had watched him in the courtroom. The breeze lifted her hair, as if in reassurance; he came closer; she did not move.

"I'm dying," he said. "I should have been dead already. I have to wear this," touching the patch on his arm, "to even stand here talking, you can't imagine the pain I'm in."

Yes I can, she thought.

"Make me a box," as he raised the bag to eye-level: fruit, tumor, sack of gold, she saw its weight in the way he held it, saw him start as she took the bag from him, red string damp with sweat from his grip, and "I told you on the phone," she said. "I can't do anything for you." She set the bag on the ground; her voice was tired. "You'd better go away now. Go home, or wherever you live. Just go away."

"Remember my workshop?" he said; now there was glass in his voice, glass and the sound of the pain—whatever was in that patch wasn't working anymore—grotesque, that sound, like a gargoyle's voice, like the voice of whatever was eating him up. "Remember what I told you there? Because of me you can do this, Alison, because of what I did, what I *gave* you . . . Now it's your turn to give to me."

"I can't give you anything," she said. Behind her, her workshop stood solid, doorframe like a box frame, holding, enclosing her life: the life she had made, piece by piece, scrap by scrap, pain and love and wonder, the boxes, the desert, and he before her now was just the bad-dream man, less real than a dream, than the shadow he made on the ground: he was nothing to her, nothing, and "I can't make something from nothing," she said, "don't you get it? All you have is what you took from other people, you don't have anything I can *use*."

His mouth moved, jaw up and down like a ventriloquist dummy's: because he wanted to speak, but couldn't? because of the pain? which pain? and "Here," she said: not because she was merciful, not because she wanted to do good for him, but because she was making a box, because it was her box, she reached out with her long, strong fingers, reached with the X-Acto knife and cut some threads from the bag, red string, thin and sinuous as veins, and "I'll keep these," she said, and closed her hand around them, said nothing as he looked at her, kept looking through the sunglasses, he took the sunglasses off and "I'm *dying*," he said finally, his voice all glass now, a glass organ pressed to a shuddering chord, but she was already turning, red threads in her palm, closing the door between them so he was left in the sun, the dying sun; night comes quickly in the desert; she wondered if he knew that.

He banged on the door, not long or fiercely; a little later she heard the truck start up again, saw its headlights, heard it leave, but by then she had already called the state police: a sober courtesy, a good citizen's compunction because her mind was busy elsewhere, was on the table with the bracelet and the varnish, the Gideon Bible and the red strings from the bag. She worked until a trooper came out to question her, then worked again when he had gone: her fingers calm on the knife and the glue gun, on the strong steel frame of the box. When she slept that night she dreamed of the desert, of long roads and empty skies, her workshop in its center lit up like a burning jewel; as she dreamed her good eye roved beneath its lid, like a moon behind the clouds.

In the morning paper it explained how, and where, they had found him, and what had happened to him when they did, but she didn't see it, she was too far even from Eventide to get the paper anymore. The trooper stopped by that afternoon, to check on how she was doing; she told him she was doing fine.

"That man's dead," he said, "stone dead. You don't have to worry about him."

"Thank you," she said. "Thank you for coming." In the box the red strings stretched from top to bottom, from the bent garage nail to the hospital bracelet, the Bible verse to the Polaroid, like roads marked on a map to show the way.

BABY

It's hot in here, and the air smells sweet, all sweet and burned, like incense. I love incense, but I can never have any; my allergies, right? Allergic to incense, to cigarette smoke, to weed smoke, to smoke in general, the smoke from the grill at Rob's Ribs, too, so goodbye to that, and no loss either, I hate this job. The butcher's aprons are like circus tents, like 3X, and those pointy paper hats we have to wear—"Smokin' Specialist," god. They look like big white dunce caps, even Rico looks stupid wearing one and Rico is *hot*. I've never seen anyone as hot as he is.

The only good thing about working here—besides Rico—is hanging out after shift, up on the rooftop while Rob and whoever swabs out the patio, and everyone jokes and flirts, and, if Rob isn't paying too much attention, me and Rico shotgun a couple of cans of Tecate or something. Then I lean as far over the railing as I can, my hands gripping tight, the metal pressing cold through my shirt; sometimes I let my feet leave the patio, just a few inches, just balancing there on the railing, in thin air . . . Andy always flips when I do it, he's all like *Oh Jani don't do that Jani you could really hurt yourself! You could fall!*

Oh Andy, I always say; Andy's like a mom or something. *Calm down, it's only gravity,* only six floors up but still, if you fell, you'd be a plate of Rob's Tuesday night special, all bones and red sauce;

smush, gross, right? But I love doing it. You can feel the wind rush up between the buildings like invisible water, stealing your breath, filling you right up to the top. It's so weird, and so choice . . . Like the feeling I always got from you, Baby.

It's kind of funny that I never called you anything else, just Baby; funny that I even found you, up there in Grammy's storage space, or crawl space, or whatever it's called when it's not really an attic, but it's just big enough to stand up in. Boxes were piled up everywhere, but mostly all I'd found were old china cup-and-saucer sets, and a bunch of games with missing pieces—Stratego, and Monopoly, and Clue; I already had Clue at home; I used to totally love Clue, even though I cheated when I played, sometimes. Well, all the time. I wanted to win. There were boxes and boxes of Grampy's old books, doctor books; one was called *Surgical Procedures and Facial Deformities* and believe me, you did *not* want to look at *that.* I flipped it open on one picture where this guy's mouth was all grown sideways, and his eyes—his eye— Anyway. After that I stayed away from the boxes of books.

And then I found you, Baby, stuffed down in a big box of clothes, chiffon scarves and unraveling lace, the cut-down skirts of fancy dresses, and old shirts like Army uniforms, with steel buttons and appliqués. At the bottom of the box were all kinds of shoes, spike heels, and a couple of satin evening bags with broken clasps. At first I thought you were a kind of purse, too, or a bag, all small and yellow and leathery. But then I turned you over, and I saw that you had a face.

Right away I liked touching you, your slick wrinkled skin, weird old-timey doll with bulgy glass eyes—they looked like glass—and a little red mouth, and fingers that could open and close; the first time you did that, fastened on me like that, it kind of flipped me out, but then I saw I could make you do it if I wanted to. And then I wanted to.

I played with you for a long time that first day, finding out what you could do, until Mommy came and bitched me out for being "missing." How big was Grammy's house? Not very, Mommy was just mad that she had to be there at all, even once a year was too much. Mommy and Grammy never really got along. *Speak English,* Mommy used to yell at her. *This is Ohio!*

So when she yelled at me I wasn't surprised: *What are you doing up here?* with the door open and the afternoon light behind her, like a witch peering into a playhouse; I was surprised at how dark it was in there, I could see *your* face perfectly fine. I knew to hide you, Baby, even though I didn't know why; I stuck you in the folds of one of the evening skirts, and *I'm just playing dress-up,* I said, but Mommy got mad at that, too: *Stay out of that stuff, all her Nazi dancehall stuff, it's all moth-eaten and disgusting. And anyway come on, we're leaving now.*

Can I take these? I said, pointing to the board games, I threw the games away when I got you home. You slept with me that first night, didn't you? You got under the blanket, and fastened on . . . It was the first time I really had it, that feeling, like when you spin yourself around to get dizzy, or when you're just about to be drunk, but a hundred times sweeter, like riding an invisible wave. I could see into things, when you did that, see into the sky, into myself, watch my own heart beat. It was so *choice.*

It's funny, too, because I never liked baby dolls, or dolls of any kind. Grammy bought me like a million Barbies, but I don't think I ever played with any of them, or the Madame Maurice dolls that anyway aren't meant to be played with, Mommy ended up selling those on eBay. But you were different. It wasn't like we were playing, I wasn't the mommy and you weren't the baby, I didn't have to dress you up, or make you walk and talk. You were pretty much real on your own . . . If I'd been a little older, I might have wondered more about that; I mean, even then I knew you weren't actually a toy. Or a "real" baby, either. You never cried, for one thing. And what you ate never made you grow.

But I knew you loved me since I got you out of that clothes box, and so you did things for me, things that I wanted you to do. Like when Alisha Parrish wrecked my Lovely Locket and wouldn't say sorry, and you puked—or whatever that was—all over her sleeping bag! That was choice. Or when I threw Mommy's car keys down the wishing well in the park, and she told me I couldn't come home until I found them. She was surprised, wasn't she, Baby?

I let you do things, too, that you wanted, like when we found that dead raccoon out by the storage shed, remember? Or the time I was so sick with the flu that the fever made me see things, and I let you fly all around the room; you were smiling, Baby, and swimming through the air. I wondered, later, how much the fever had to do with it, and for a long time after, I kept watching, to see if you would smile again, or fly . . . It was kind of like having a pet, a pet who was also a friend.

And a secret, because I knew without even thinking about it that I could never show you to anyone, not sleepover friends or school friends or anyone, that you were only meant for me. You knew it, too. And you were happy, you didn't need anyone but me anyway.

For sure Mommy's never seen you—Mommy doesn't even go into my room—but Roger knew about you, or knew *something*; remember Roger? With the mustache and bald head? He used to look at me weird, like he was sad or something, and once or twice he asked me if I was OK: *You doing all right, Jani? You feeling all right?*

I'm fine.

Anything you want to talk about? If you're not—feeling good, or anything, you can always talk to your mom about it. Roger didn't know Mommy very well. And he didn't last very long.

Definitely Flaco knew about you, I don't know how but he did. He finally caught us in the hallway, in the Pensacola house, when Mommy was at the gym, he popped out of the bathroom like he'd been standing there waiting, and *So there's your Santeria toy,* he said. *Come on, Jani, let's see it.*

He smelled like aftershave, and skunky weed; he was smiling. In the dusty hallway light, you looked yellower than normal; I could feel the heat coming off you, like it does when you're hungry. I tried to hide you under my arm.

It's just a doll, I said.

Ah, that ain't no dolly, girl, come on. That's a bat-boy! A familiar. My Uncle Felix had one, he called it Little Felix. We used to say it was the Devil's little brother. Flaco was still smiling; the skunk-weed smell was burning my throat. *He bites when you tell him to, don't he? Does anything you tell him to.*

I didn't know what to say. I didn't know how he knew. "Familiar"? With what? The Devil's little brother. Family. You were squirming under my arm, I couldn't tell if you were angry or afraid.

They can do some crazy shit, familiars. Come on, I won't tell your mama. Let me see—and he tried to make a grab for you, he put his hand on you, and *Stop it!* I said.

Let me see, girl!

You stop it, or I'll tell Mommy you tried to touch me, I'll say you tried to touch me under my shirt.

I wouldn't never— That's a sick kind of lie, Jani! but we both knew that Mommy would believe me, Flaco was pretty much a straight-up man-whore from Day One. He let us go then, didn't he, Baby? And he never said anything about you again, to me or to Mommy, even though I let you do things to him, once or twice—OK, more than that, but whatever, he was passed-out high when you did it, and anyway he deserved it, right? And even though he knew—he had to know—how it happened, those bites, he never said a word.

Flaco moved out that Christmas Eve and took all the presents with him, his and ours: *A real class act,* Mommy said, and then she threw a big Christmas party to celebrate, and to get more presents. Mommy said she was tired of Flaco's drama anyway, and really tired of Pensacola, and so was I.

So I hid you in my backpack and we moved back to Ohio—Bay Ridge—and I hated it, hated middle school, hated the girls who made fun of my jeans and called me a trashburger and a slut; I was like eleven years old, how much of a slut could I have been? Even in Bay

Ridge? In Ohio you wrinkled up like a raisin, and you barely moved at all—I think it was too cold for you there, I don't think you can, like, process the cold. In Pensacola you always smelled a little bit funky, like an old sneaker left in a closet, or a dog's chew toy, but at least you could get around. Once or twice in Bay Ridge, you were so stiff and so still in my backpack that I thought you were, you know, dead, and I cried, Baby. I really, really cried.

When we moved again, down to Clearwater, things got better; you liked it better here, too, at least at first, right? It was warm again, for one thing. And I started high school, which is a lot more fun than middle school, and our house is a lot nicer, too: there are two bathrooms, and the solarium with the hot tub, even if it leaks, and the home office where Mommy works, she's an online "consultant" now—

What kind of a consultant?

I'm a relationship counselor.

What kind of relationships?

—but the more I asked, the madder she got, all pinched up around the mouth until she looked like Grammy; and really I don't care, right? At least we have money now, at least there are no more boy-friends wandering all over the house in their tighty-whities. Not hers, anyway . . . The first time I did it with a boy, you knew some-how, didn't you, Baby? When I got back from the Freshman Spring Fling, you smelled all over my hands and face, and then you went all stiff at the side of the bed, and you didn't want to fasten on, you wouldn't until I made you.

And when I woke up the next morning you weren't there, even though I looked all over, and Mommy yelled at me for being late to school, *I'm not going to call in for you again, Jani, I mean it!* All day I thought, *Oh god, what if Mommy finds Baby?* I couldn't imagine what she would do to you, or to me. Kick me out, or who knows what Mommy would do.

I was pretty scared, and pretty mad, when I got home. Mommy was sleeping, so I tore apart the house again, and when finally I found you, curled up behind the washer—where Mommy could have seen you in a second, if she ever bothered to look, if she ever bothered to do a load of clothes—*Where were you?* I said. I think I shook you a little, or a lot. *Where the hell were you?*

You just rolled your glass eyes at me and didn't make a sound. All sad and cold and stiff, like—like beef jerky or something, you were *nasty.* So I stuffed you into the old backpack, I threw you into the back of the closet, and I almost didn't let you out. Almost. Except I finally did, and I let you fasten on, too. And you were happy, Baby, I could tell, that night it was like both of us were flying. After that, no matter what I did or who I hooked up with, or even if I didn't come home all night, you never ran away again. I knew you needed me, then, more than I needed you. And I realized that I didn't really need you much at all.

But that was going to happen anyway, right? because really, the older I get, the more I can do for myself, and the less I need the things that you can do—and the things I can't get, you can't either, I mean I'm not going to send you into the liquor store, right? *Crawl up into the cold case, get me a six-pack of Tecate, Baby!* And even the fastening-on—even though we still do it, and I still like it, I can get to that place without you, now. Driving really fast, smoking up and then drinking—it's mostly the same feeling, not as pure or as . . . as good as with you, but I can be with other people when I get it. People like Bobby, or Justin, or Colin. Or Rico. Especially Rico.

I told Rico about you, Baby. I didn't plan to beforehand, but I did. We were in the storage room—Rob said to go unpack the napkins, there must have been like fifty boxes—but instead we were joking around, and flirting, and I was trying to think of ways to keep him talking; I wanted to stay that way, the two of us alone together, for as long as I could. I wanted to show him that I'm—different, from Carmen, and Kayla, and those other girls, those pervy night shift girls, I wanted him to know something about me. To be—familiar with me. So I told him about you.

At first it seemed like he was impressed: *Whoa, that's some crazy shit. How'd your grandma get something like that?*

She was like in a war, or something. "Her Nazi dancehall stuff"— that's creepy to think of, actually, because I'd never really thought about where you came from, or how Grampy got you. Or who might have—made you, or whatever. You weren't born like normal, that's for sure.

You saying the doll's, like, alive, Jani? For real?

Not alive-alive. But he moves around and everything. You should see him when he eats!

Rico was smiling—*That's so crazy*—but I couldn't tell if he thought it was cool-crazy or weird-crazy; I couldn't tell if I'd just made a big mistake. And then Rob came looking for the napkins, and bitched us both out for taking so long: *What were you guys doing in there anyway?* Everyone laughed, Rico, too. Later on, I asked Rico if he wanted to come over and use the hot tub, but he said he was busy, and maybe we could just hang out at work instead. So I guess you can't help me with Rico, Baby, after all.

And even if I wanted to ask Grammy about you, or give you back, I can't: because she's gone, right, she finally died in that hospice in Ohio. Mommy said she found out too late to be able to go to the funeral, but she sure got there fast enough for the will, she must have taken half the furniture from that house. I wonder what happened to all of that other stuff, those old clothes, and the medical books . . . Maybe I should have asked Flaco about you, back when I had the chance.

The thing is, Rico finally said yes, Baby, when we were up on the roof last night, I was leaning over the railing and he was standing next to me, and I told him that Friday was my last night at Rob's Ribs, that I was quitting to go back to school; it's online school, but still, Mommy said I could quit working if I take at least one class, and anyway I didn't tell him that part. *I'd like to, like, be with you,* I said to Rico. *Before I go.*

And he smiled so you could see all his dimples, god he is so hot.

And then he said, *OK, wild child, how about I come over tomorrow? I have to drive up to Northfield, but I can be over by midnight.* Mommy might be home, but Mommy doesn't bother me, she doesn't care what I do. So I said, *Absolutely,* I said, *Come over whenever you want.*

But the thing is, you can't be there, Baby, I don't want you to be there, I don't want Rico to ask, *Hey where's that crazy doll?* And if he does, I want to be able to say *Oh that? Oh, I don't have that any more.*

But I don't want to—to bury you alive in some old clothes box, you didn't like it the first time, right, when Grammy or Grampy stuck you in there? I know you didn't. Just like you don't like living in my old backpack with the April-May-Magic stickers and the black plaid bows, stuffed way down in the very back of my closet, behind the Princess Jasmine bedspread. When I take you out to feed you, now, you just—look at me. I hate the way you looking at me feels . . . I'm just too old to play with dolls.

It really does smell like incense in here, like hot, sweet wood burning. No one's supposed to mess with the smokers—Rob does that himself, all the cleaning—but Andy helps the cooks load, and he says it's not that hard; he's going to help me, too. He doesn't know what's in the backpack, when he asked I just said *Memories,* and he nodded. Andy will do what I want him to do; like you, Baby. They keep the smokers at, like, 250 degrees, but it can go a lot higher, a lot hotter, I bet it won't even hurt. Not like falling off the roof, right? No Tuesday night special, just ash, and gone . . . I'm going to throw in that stupid "Smokin' Specialist" hat, too.

I wonder if you knew that's why I let you fasten on, last night, for one last time? You seemed so happy to get out of the closet, and the backpack, to be close to me again. I'd take you out again to say goodbye, right here behind the shelves, but if I look at you, your sad glass eyes, then I won't do it, maybe. Maybe. But I can't keep you forever anyway, and Rico will be over tonight.

The smoke smell is everywhere in here, digging a barbed-wire itch in my throat, in my chest, it makes me cough. Afterward, when Andy's done, I'm going to go up onto the roof and lean over the railing, let my feet dangle and feel like I'm flying. Flying and crying, for you and for me: because I *am* crying, Baby, just a little, because I'm going to miss you a lot.

VELOCITY

Linden; aspen; maple; ash. A postcard setting, slant light and falling leaves, gravel switchback leading to a KEEP OUT gate, more sentry trees, a clustering clot of outbuildings—spare metal sheds, an emptied four-car garage. At the heart of the property, alone in bloody maple drift, stands an incongruous house, a hard-edged, sumptuous folly that at first glance seems neglected: dusty windows, drawn blinds, heavy bicycle chain hung across the door, front door. The chain is old; the locks—two locks—are bright and new.

Everywhere, broken bicycles.

• • •

Q: So what you're saying is that the process is equal to the art produced? That *how* is, essentially, *why*?

A: No, I—*no*. I'm saying the way I make my art can't be separated out from what I make, like a, like an egg white, OK? Christ, where do they find you people? I'm *saying* that when I aim a bike at a tree and crash it, that that's *part* of what the piece is about. The velocity, where it hits, how it fragments—every time it's different, none of them end up the same—

Q: Yet the process is identical. Are you willing to discuss what informs the process itself?

A: Give me a hand here. [His right arm is in a sling. He needs help to light another cigarette.] I have no idea what you just said.

Q: More simply, then: why do you make art by running bicycles into trees? What . . . drives your particular mode of self-expression?

[No answer.]

Q: Are you at all willing to discuss—

A: I thought you wanted to talk about my work. I thought this was—

Q: But art is a product of a human imagination, a human mind, a human body; especially your art, Mr. Vukovich. You shattered your arm while making this latest sculpture, you—

A: I don't have to listen to this shit.

[Break.]

• • •

The house was built in the early 1970s, an austere and "modern" fantasia of brushed metal and glass block. It has eight rooms, three of them very large: the living or reception room, which takes up most of the first floor; the dining room, and the master bedroom; the rest are markedly, almost painfully, small. All are spare, as in a monastery or zendo: low teak tables, white futons, stainless steel appliances. All the windows have identical white paper blinds. All the walls are red. The dining table is laid with service for nine.

• • •

Q: Were you pleased with the Ortega installation?

A: Sure. Mary was great, she always does a great job.

Q: She's been your dealer for quite some time now, correct? Since you—returned from Arizona?

[No answer.]

Q: Mary Ortega is well-known—almost notorious—for her attraction to, let's say, a certain type of painful art. Art that expresses hurtful or violent emotions, art that specifically—

A: Jesus Christ, you're not going to get off it, are you? You didn't come here to talk about my work at all, all you want is to talk about my goddamned father, isn't that right? [His uninjured arm is trembling badly, almost theatrically.] There are plenty of articles about him, why don't you go read them? Why don't you do a search? You'll be fucking buried in—

Q: Your father was a famous man. And since his death—

A: He didn't *die*, he killed himself.

Q: —forgive me, since his suicide, you've lived here alone in the house that he designed and commissioned, making art that graphically recalls the manner of his death. Mr. Vukovich, I don't mean to be unkind or impertinent, but when a father commits suicide by driving into a tree, and his son's art does nothing but recreate that moment, one cannot help but speculate that these things are intimately related. One cannot—

A: You think it's some kind of, of *tribute*, is that it? Jesus! You think that I—

Q: What I think is unimportant. What matters are your thoughts, your ideas about the—

A: I think you better pack up your little briefcase and go. That's what I think.

• • •

The Red House, as it is called, is a kind of singularity, and as such there was for a time a great demand for tours: from architecture and design professionals, professors and students, historians interested in its provenance, cultural anthropologists, as well as all the lesser hordes that treasure celebrity and wealth. After the owner's spectacular and graphic suicide, the estate fell hostage to legal squabbles between his first wife and current partner; the dispute was eventually resolved in the wife's favor, but by that time she herself had died, in a fire at her horse farm in Truro. The couple's only surviving relative, a son, himself an artist, came into possession of the house and immediately discontinued all public tours. It was believed that he was living on the property, but his attorney's office would not confirm that this was true.

• • •

Q: Perhaps it would—perhaps we might talk a little about your early work. In Switzerland, you—

A: If you want to talk about him, I don't care. No, really. Let's do it. I don't give a fuck. [Speech today is slurred. He seems to have difficulty sitting upright. The cast has been removed, but he is still wearing a sling.]

Q: You're sure? I don't want to—All right, then. Your father, Edwin Vukovich—

A: The Prince of Darkness. Ed, to his friends. Of which he had none. Not even my mother. My mother used to warn me not to tell him anything: where I lived, what I was doing. If you tell him, he can use it, she always said. Don't give him anything he can use.

Q: He was an architect—

A: Architect manqué. Everyone thinks he designed the Red House, you know, but that's not true. He got this kid from RISD to make some drawings, and then he— Anyway when I was at school, everyone thought he was like some big influence on me. Influence! He never even saw one of my installations, not one.

Q: And yet perhaps his influence was felt in other ways—?

A: Yeah. Like cancer. When I was in Berlin—fuck Berlin, when I was in *Sedona*, these people would show up out of the blue, these—sideshow freaks— Once, at one of my openings, this woman came up to me, she had all these pictures she wanted me to look at. Pictures of him, you know, him and her and— He was like an insect, you know? a praying mantis or a scorpion or something. He had no idea what it was like to be human and he didn't care.

Q: Yet he was quoted more than once as saying how proud he was of your work. He even tried to purchase one of your—

A: Right. *Heresy*, it was one of the first things I did at Mary's. It was like a ski run, with these little— You've seen it, right?

Q: Photographs of it, yes. It was an extraordinary installation. The almost insane sense of speed, of uncontrolled velocity—

A: Yeah. A good piece. But Mary's smart, you know. She gave him a lot of sweet talk, but she wouldn't let him have the piece. Just like my mother said. Like voodoo. Skin cells, little bits of bone . . . They didn't tell you how he used to beat my mother, did they? He'd go through her closet, take out one of her little chain belts, Gucci, whatever, and just go to town. I used to try to get between them, make him stop . . . When I got older, I bought a gun. I actually thought it would help! But I didn't need a gun, what I needed was, was silver bullets—

Q: Mr. Vukovich—

A: —or a stake through his heart. Right? Isn't that how you kill the devil? But that's the thing, you know? That's the whole fucking problem, because you can't kill the devil, not ever. Not with stakes or crosses or lawyers or—

Q: Mr. Vukovich, if this is distressing you, we—

A: *Christ*, my arm hurts.

[Break.]

• • •

In the room that was formerly used as the laundry, the appliances have been removed, and a small living space constructed, a scruffy human patch on the glass and steel. The items inside—a blue down sleeping bag, worn and leaking feathers; a Coleman stove; a bed tray; a scuffed plastic washtub—suggest an extended habitation. A shelf has been affixed three feet from the floor, just above the bundled sleeping bag, in easy reach of anyone lying below. On this shelf is a pink drugstore flashlight, an inhaler, an ashtray, a Remington automatic shotgun, its barrel sheared almost to the nub, and a copy of *Art in America*. Above the shelf is a crucifix, olivewood, immensely old. The corpus has been replaced with two bent roofing nails.

• • •

A: When I was working on *Acrimony*, I kept getting these phone calls. At first I thought it was just crank stuff, some dumbshit breathing on the phone, once or twice I even talked to him. Just, you know, are you having fun, asshole? Mary said it was creepy and that I ought to call the cops, or something, but I didn't. I thought it was kind of funny . . . But then he started calling me at home.

Q: You were staying—?

A: At home. At the Red House.

Q: I don't— The number is unlisted?

A: There're no phones in the house. No phone jacks, even. But I'd hear it ring, and ring, and ring, it'd go on for fucking hours. Sometimes I'd go sit outside just to get away from the sound. Sometimes I'd sleep outside . . . Then I started sleeping at the gallery, in Mary's office. Which helped— You should see your face. You look like the cat that just ate shit.

Q: [Silence.]

A: When I finally got the show up, the calls stopped. Like he was trying to fuck me over, right? Get me to stop working—

A: Who?

Q: Who do you think? Mary said I was working too hard, you know, or taking too much speed— Wait, erase that. But if it was the speed then how come I never heard it *unless* I was working? The phone, and the knocking on the windows—I had them come and trim the branches, just hack them away from the house—I mean I knew what it was but I wanted to be sure, right? And I was right.

It wasn't trees or shrubs or branches, it was goddamn *knocking* and it was him. Just like the phone was him. Just like the guy at the bike shop, the one I always use, right? Now he won't sell me any more bikes, he says it's too dangerous. Dangerous! To him, he means. Because he knows. Because he gets into people's heads, like poison gas, or something—like he did to my mother, I watched him do it. She used to be, she was so . . . And then he killed her. I know it was him, there's no way that barn burned by itself. And he got Teo, too—

Q: Teo?

A: Her horse. They found them together, she was all— And then he tried to do it to me. In Sedona, Berlin, where-the-fuck-ever, doesn't matter, never did. You think being dead is a *problem* for him? Hell no! It just makes it *easier*, you know? It just makes everything easier.

Q: Mr. Vukovich—Mr. Vukovich, when you were working on *Calefaction*, Mary Ortega was quoted as—

A: Don't change the subject! Don't change the subject! You said you wanted to talk about him, well that's what we're talking about! Are you afraid? Is that it? "Speak of the devil and the devil appears"? But he's already here. He's already right—

Q: Mr. Vukovich—

A: Stop *saying* that.

[Break.]

• • •

As per the trust, the Red House and its grounds are serviced on a seasonal schedule. Mowing, raking, bundling brush, blowing snow; repairing the depredations of weather; replacing the furnace filter, caulking the cracks; there is a lavish budget set aside for these things and they are always faithfully performed.

The former laundry room is rigorously avoided, unless there is actual damage within it needing repair. When the lawn crews arrive the broken and discarded bicycles are carefully removed to the garage; before the crews leave, the parts are restored to their earlier approximate positions. This is not part of the trust's directions but there is a sizable rider to the maintenance contract to insure that these things are done, or not done. Money, as always, is neutral, and efficient in its demands.

• • •

Q: You have a new show opening soon?

A: I'm not— Yeah. I guess. I don't know the dates, you better ask Mary.

Q: It's titled *The Erl King,* is that right?

A: Yeah. Mary doesn't like it, the title, but that's just too fucking bad. I know what I'm doing.

Q: Mr. Vukovich, you— Would you rather not continue today? You seem very—

A: I don't *seem* like anything. I *am.* You would be too. Maybe you will be. He doesn't like me to talk to you, you know. So I was up all fucking night last night, listening to him crawl through the pipes—I was afraid to, to take a shit, you know? Because what if he decided to crawl inside me? I wouldn't put it past him. I wouldn't put anything past him.

Q: Perhaps we ought to reschedule our—

A: Perhaps you ought to shut the fuck up and listen to what I'm telling you . . . listen . . . did you hear that?

Q: Hear what? I didn't—

A: Oh yes you did. You wanted to know all about my art, my homage to his suicide or whatever you called it—

Q: I—

A: —like it's some weird Oedipal thing, but the fact is, I just have to keep doing it, you know, until it sticks. Until it *works.* Man, you think I like to keep doing the same piece over and over? Think I like hurting myself? breaking my arm? *and* my shin, and my

fucking heel bone, which still hurts, they never did set it right—
But I have to. I don't need that guy at the bike shop, I can order
anything I want, they don't even have to know it's me. Because
if he's in the pipes today, where will he be tomorrow? Huh? Up
my ass, that's where, and crawling out of my mouth! You think
I need that? I'd rather break my neck on a bike! I'd rather—

Q: Mr. Vukovich, you're very upset. We'd better stop this now, we'd
better just—

A: You see this gun?

Q: I—oh my God. Look, I'm, I'm leaving now. I can't—

A: No, take it. Take it! And hold it on me. Like this. Like this! *Hold
it!* . . . that's right. You sit there and you hold it. And if he crawls
out of my mouth, you shoot him. Hear me? Shoot the mother-
fucker in the head.

• • •

Because of the way the Red House is constructed, because of its
placement on the grounds, and the arrangement of the trees and
shrubs around it, it owns a peculiar radiance in the early evening
sun, a deep and affecting glow as if the house were lit from within,
like fire in the depths of a jewel. Visitors are not always aware of
this phenomenon, and are sometimes confused by the house's name,
seeing only its gunmetal-gray-and-glass exterior. But if one arrives
at almanac sundown, the house will indeed be glowing, as hot and
red and chambered as a beating heart.

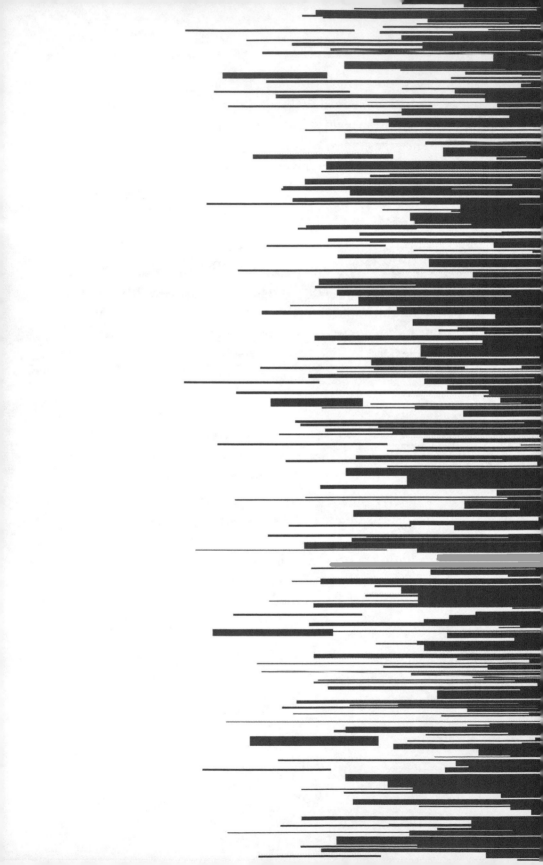

DOWNTOWN

CLUBS

In Lisi's bathroom: whorling shells on the shower curtain, pink shower curtain, pink cosmetic smell, and she had, she said, done nothing but perms all day, nothing but put rods in hair and take them out again, stiff and juicy, and now those chapped hands surgeon—deft, swabbing and dipping, and "What're you doing," I said, perched on the toilet to watch her, talking just to say something, make some noise. "What're you—"

"I'm putting on my face, what's it look like I'm doing?" Long nails: a wrapped and lacquered caucasian beige, half were real and half were not; I could always tell the fakes, they broke off in bed, stuck brittle in the pillowcase, in my hair for spoor and souvenir although we didn't spend much time in bed anymore, Lisi and me; I was her chew toy now, club buddy, confidant; I was not there to replace Martin or even act as if I could.

"So where are we going?" I said; she didn't answer. "You want to try Foxhunt's?"

"I don't care," which was a lie; the itinerary was always hers, this other was just a dance we did, something else done to please her: not possible because she could not be pleased, not by me: it was Martin she wanted, Martin or nobody, and I was nobody now. So we did the club thing together, six nights a week and Sundays off for good behavior: Foxhunt's and the Tunnel, BillyAnne or Panixx, the night mapped to her configurations, and I was pretty much just along for the ride, to pay for drinks and cabs, window-dressing boyfriend if she needed to get rid of somebody, some other nobody come sniffing for her blonde hair and her crotch. Sometimes—not often but often enough—she got rid of me, ersatz escort but always very nicely, very discreetly, tugging me by the sleeve, and "Listen," she'd say, her lips to my ear, "listen, I think I'm going to stick around," my signal to get lost and I usually did, although once in a while I'd say "Sure, go ahead," then stay just to tease her, just to watch the other guy's face when he caught me lurking at the bar or pissing purposefully in the men's room like I just had to drain off this last half-liter before I came out to kick his ass. Although— and to my credit, I think; I hope—I never seriously cramped her style; if she wanted to get laid by some asshole in leather jeans, some other non-Martin, why not? At bedrock it was nothing and nothing was what she wanted.

And afterwards the spiel, the dish, *tell me all about it in the morning*, some ratbag cafe two doors down from her place and she'd buy me New Orleans-style pastries, beignets, and "He was a wild man," she'd say, laughing, mouth white with powdered sugar, ghost lips, or "Dead meat" with a frown, a manufactured pout, but how be angry when it all proved to her what she already knew, wanted to know? and my function then was to listen and make little comments, laugh if it was funny; sometimes it was; even Martin had been one of the funny ones. At first. A lot of things that happened to Lisi were funny at first.

Now: "How about Shadowbox?" and her shrug at my suggestion, wiping at her eyelids, her throat, head tilted to show the line, chin-tip to nipple, smooth and clean; and she had gained back most of the weight lost on her special diet, speedball-and-cigarette purge learned at work, one of the other stylists whose boyfriend was a bike messenger, winged death: 90 pounds and chronic cramps, her hair coming out in clumps before I stopped her, made her stand in front of a mirror: "You look like shit," I said to her careless shrug. "You look thirty-five," and "I do not," but it got her attention, got her to start eating again: fruit shakes mostly, and soup, I brought her lots of carryout wonton and *czarnina*, she couldn't keep anything else down. Wrapped in her pink patchwork quilt, sucking on a straw: *I'm cold*, she kept saying, *isn't it cold in here?* Looking at me like a refugee, no makeup, clutching her cup of soup; like taking care of my grandma, my auntie on crutches, those same claw hands. *Isn't it cold in here?*

"Anyway," flicking on mascara, too close to the mirror, "Shadowbox is dead on Fridays. What about," and that sideways look, I knew what she was going to say and she knew I knew, knew what I thought, too, but said it anyway: "What about Punch'n'Julie's?"

Silence: my shrug unsuccessful because what was it to me anyway? and finally "All right," I said, "sure, if that's what you want," and off into the bedroom then, closet-door noises, drawers opening to close, and me still on the toilet, ankles crossed and resigned, and "Okay," she said, "okay, I'm ready." Short black skirt, black shirt buttoned decorous to the neck, stirrup boots. "Let's go."

"You look pretty," I said. "Really hot."

That long lipstick curve: did she believe me? "Martin says—used to say," as if he had died, "that compliments undermine a person's self-confidence, that you shouldn't need someone else to tell you, you should just know when you look good."

"Really?" I said. "What utter bullshit," but her face closed, the wrong thing to say even though it was true. In the cab she tried to give me some pills: really cool, she said, like speed but without the crash, but "Without the crash," I said, "it's not speed. Anyway you're not supposed to be taking any kind of speed, right? That's what made that hole in your belly, right?"

Sullen, one shoulder hitched high to make a wall, keep me out, shut me up. "This isn't the same shit. Besides, if you can't be happy sometimes why even bother?"

No answer to that, or none I knew, and so I said nothing at all, sat watching out the window, traffic lurch and crawl and two guys arguing at a red light, one waving a magazine in the other's face, waving and shouting, and closer we could hear "Asshole! Asshole!" The cabbie changed the radio station, blurry reggae to Cuban pop and "Go that way," I called through the shield, pointing to the right. "That way, okay?"

"Okay," he said without looking either at me or in the direction I'd pointed. Lisi dry-swallowed the pills. The Cuban pop turned to news and the cabbie shut it off.

• • •

Barely ten o'clock and a line already, inside a line at the bar, all the tables were full but "Tommy, hey," pinwheeling her arm, "hey Tommy," and there he was, Tommy-from-work, blond curls and baggy tweed shorts, and it turned out he'd saved us seats, ringside view right below the giant sign: WELCOME TO PUNCH'N'JULIE'S! in day-glo letters, beneath which capered a stylized raccoon in bike helmet and boxing gloves, club mascot, someone's idea of a joke. A stupid joke. It used to be called SQUARED CIRCLE which was at least a better name, but last year some kind of lawsuit, blood and thunder and the place changed hands, changed signs, new waivers and a new paint job—yellow and aqua, gag—but the ring was still there, bright lights and regulation ropes and, now, ringside sports fan, heavy better, take two people—anybody, men or women though it was mostly women now—and stick them in that ring, the crowd around them, staring and shouting and banging their bottles, betting under the tables, in the pisser, strictly cash: two-to-one, ten-to-one, even odds. Now give those two in the ring—who stand sweating, smiling, or pretending to smile, pretending they can see their friends yelling like ten-year-olds from the dark, past the overhead dazzle—give them cheap orange bike helmets and foam-rubber aluminum-cored bats, and start the clock running for a three-minute bout. Score points for every hit, double points for a knockdown and offer a cash prize for the winner, two hundred dollars and the loser gets a free drink. One drink.

Anyone can play.

Video screens showing clips of old prize fights, snippets of boxing movies to an all-purpose Top 40 soundtrack, bass-heavy and too loud, and why did she even bother asking me where I wanted to go, why not just say we're meeting someone at Punch'n'Julie's? Because she knew I knew? Because even she was embarrassed, to be following Martin around, hanging out at his hangouts, peeking through the crowd to see if he was there? and "Hey hey," Tommy's atonal cry, he always sounded like his head was either hollow or too full. "Lisi, hey. Have a seat." Half a pitcher of beer on the table, dark beer. "What're you drinking?"

"Your beer," I said. "Got a glass?" but he pretended as if he hadn't heard me, couldn't see me, poured his own glass full, and Lisi ordered from the barmaid, double shot of Black Ice and for me a beer, any beer, cheap and flat and yellow, and I watched her, just very openly watched her, because I knew she couldn't help herself, she had to look, she had to see: head swiveling like a turret, cheap toy, is he here? Is he? and Tommy said something, lost in the speaking as a bell rang, sharp through the music, and at once the cheers as into the ring came a short dark woman in a green spandex getup, spill of braids elaborate beneath the cheesy orange helmet, and behind her a puffy blonde in thigh-cut shorts and running bra, smile of dopey glee, and "Let's welcome tonight's first sluggers," the hooting female PA voice, "Marva-and-Andrea!" and the cheering escalated, Tommy on his feet and waving, Lisi facing away from the action, where is he? and in the ring they were getting the Marquis-of-Queensberry spiel, thirty-second lecture on the rules from a bored-looking guy in a raccoon T-shirt: the dark woman, Marva, standing head-cocked and listening, bright green bat on her shoulder, while blonde Andrea seemed to be hearing instructions from the voices in her head. "She's fucked up," Tommy howled, "look at her"—until another bell, louder still, past louder screams, and the countdown time begun: 3:00 on the ringside clock, Andrea turning to wave at the crowd as Marva in one fierce pivot hit her right in the belly with the bat.

And Tommy's bellow: "Fuck!" but in beginning it was already over, Andrea dazed and battered at leisure from one end of the ring to the other by Marva and her day-glo bat, who was aiming, I saw, for points rather than damage: fifty, a hundred, two-fifty, and as the clock timed out, she even pulled her last blow, sent it wheeling harmless over Andrea's head, Andrea who by now was bent at the waist, clutching herself and: "—winner of Round One—" shouted over the PA as Andrea took two half-steps toward her corner then paused to turn, like a step in a dance, to spray vomit all over, gouts and spatters toward the tables like a fireman spraying a blaze.

She didn't get her free drink, either.

• • •

"What a farce," Tommy moody with his beer. "She never even hit her."

"Why don't you try it?" I said. Lisi had gone from the table; to the ladies' room, she said. With a detour around the club, make the circuit, get a clue. "Get on up there and show us how it's done."

"Oh, no," shaking his head, reaching for cigarettes, Lisi's cigarettes. "No, I don't believe in it, any of it. It's a ritualized violence thing, and I'm not into that at all, I don't even play sports . . . Anyway the whole thing's just a metaphor," as if I might not be smart enough to get the joke. "It's a substitute for all the shit that goes on out there," two fingers flicking toward not the club around us, would-be competitors, bat-jockeys in jerk helmets, but presumably the street beyond it, the city. "Just a way to let off some steam."

"Otherwise we'd all be roaming the streets with foam-rubber bats, huh?"

"Right, you're right," as solemnly as if I was, and what if I was, what if we both were, so what? It was still stupid, he was still stupid, and I still wanted to go home: "I'm going to take off," said to Lisi, returned, big eyes open at me, and "Why?" she said as if she cared. Why? Because this is stupid. Because Tommy is stupid. Because you— "I'm tired," I said, and "See you for coffee?" more than half-distracted, less than half a smile, because she didn't need me now and close to five the next morning, jerked from sleep by the buzz of the phone: Lisi drunk, exceedingly drunk and wanting me to guess who had come to the club that night, who had showed up after I left, who had had the nerve to stroll in with some stupid overdressed bimbo slut, and "Martin," I said, but she didn't hear me, didn't want to hear, only wanted to talk: "No, it was Martin!" and into the rant expected, how much she hated him, hated to see him and then something else, something about a comment he'd made, some stupid crack, and "So I did it," she said, "I signed up. I just fucking well signed myself up, so he can just shut his fucking little mouth."

"For what?" Outside somebody was yelling, rhythmic as the sound of a barking dog: hey hey hey. Police siren. I had to be up in three hours. "What'd you—"

"To play," she said, and started laughing. "I signed up to play."

• • •

At first I said I wouldn't go, it was stupid as well as ugly, she was only doing it for Martin's sake which was the worst reason in the world, and "No no no," earnestly, "you have it all backwards, I'm doing it to spite him, see, he thinks I can't—": the same thing completely but she didn't see it, couldn't see it; if I had stayed, that night, stayed to stop her, but "At least get a better helmet," I said, "at least you can—"

"Tommy's getting me one," and Tommy of course witness to the confrontation, Tommy who apparently thought the whole thing was a great idea, and I spent the next week working to convince her it was not: at Dixie's and the Foxhunt, Club Jitters and Po' Boy and Planet Automatic, buying her gin-and-juices, arguing with her in cabs and on foot, all the way home from her job: pink-and-black storefront, broken glass a brown glitter before the door, and maybe Tommy was right, maybe it would be cathartic, but "Maybe you'll get your head knocked off," I said, hooking arms with her, pushing past two guys with broken tambourines and a sign that said GULF WAR VETS. "Did you ever think of that?"

"Don't be a pessimist."

"I'm not. I'm just being realistic," but she wasn't listening, she didn't care and so: gin and juice and diatribes on Martin, she was going to kick some ass, she kept saying it, going to kick some ass and from my weariness I thought, *Why not*; let her because she was past listening, had never listened much to me anyway and why should she? Non-man, non-Martin, and so: see her now in Tommy's black and silver bike helmet, storm trooper chin strap, and his wrist guards, too, black leotard getup, and "She looks hot," Tommy yelled in my ear, yelled past the cheers and whistles, drunk guys calling *Hey baby!* and "Don't you think she looks hot?" but she wasn't looking at me, was scanning the club, squint in the dazzle and pour of the lights, and I had tried, all the way there, gin in the cab and three of the pills, speed growling like gears in her belly, but look at her, look at her now: head back, chin up, Miss Babe Ruth next to some health-club bitch with a buzzcut and the PA sounding her name: "—sluggers, Donna and Lisa!" and "It's Lisi," Tommy's howl, "you assholes it's LISI!" but they didn't hear because no one could hear, no one was listening, and see her look, see that scan dart and stop, stop dead, and I turned as if caught on the string of her vision, pulled taut and unwilling to see what I knew I would see: Martin there at the back, by the bar, Martin with some woman in black and white, and the briefest nod, wry salute to Lisi in the ring who pretended not to notice but whose body grew noticeably tighter, muscle and bone, gladiator arch, and "Good luck!" Tommy cried as the bell rang, "Lisi good luck!" and I turned, helpless proxy to watch Martin take a long and thoughtful drink, then turn his head to watch his girlfriend, bored already, make her way across the bar.

And Lisi leaping predator, stunning the other woman with a blow across the back: vicious and inexpert, so hard the other fell and points lit up on the scoreboard; another bell rang and Lisi hit her again, this time in the stomach, muscles and sinew, bone and bone, and hit her again, driving her back against the ropes, hit her harder, and Tommy was screaming, head back and screaming, and everyone was screaming, laughter and cheers as more points rang up, Lisi mouth-open and breathing like an animal, speed glare, and the other woman made some small attempts, feeble swing here and there, but it was Lisi's game and she knew it, they both knew it: relentless that advance as if it was—I knew—Martin she battered, Martin she struck: sweat on her back, on her arms and her face in that Noh grimace, squared mouth, and Tommy chanting, laughing, banging his bottle on the table, and I wanted to scream at her, climb into the ring and grab her arms and stop it, stop it, but I did nothing, said nothing, only turned in my seat to see, observe Martin at the bar: Martin who was barely watching, Martin who as I watched turned away—

—and I was out of my seat then, no conscious plan, and through the crowd, all faced away, faced toward the ring and the ringing bells, and "Mike," Martin said to me, next to me, an almost-friendly nod past his girlfriend's gaze indifferent, "hey Mike, how's it going?" Black jeans, black leather jacket, one arm around his girlfriend's waist; Lisi in the ring, and "Fine," I said, my heart in curious motion, red surge in my chest as the scoreboard bell rang again; two guys on Martin's other side laughed out loud. "I'm fine. How do you like the show?"

"What, Lisi?" and his shrug and smile, something about a joke and a challenge, he'd never meant her to take it all so seriously, she was such a serious person, and then something said to the girlfriend, something private in her ear, and as she laughed—

I hit him

—without thinking, my body in motion, hit him once and then again as his girlfriend shrieked and threw her drink at me, glass and liquid, and I hit him again—in the face, in the mouth, in the teeth—before someone, bouncers, pulled me off and away, pulled me outside where they pushed me against the wall and punched me, chest and belly where no bruises would show.

• • •

Three minutes is a very long time.

• • •

Thursday, this coming Thursday, is my court date; the lawyer they gave me thinks it won't be a problem, simple assault with no priors, *Romeo defense,* and he laughed a little but stopped when I didn't laugh along. I don't think it's funny; I don't think any of it is funny. Last night at the Vault I saw Lisi, with Tommy; she was drunk and they were dancing, and kissing; Martin was there, too, with a different girlfriend, but he didn't see me. Lisi didn't see me either, or if she did, she pretended not to.

It's not as if I liked it, any of it, hitting him; hurting him. But I wouldn't have stopped if they hadn't stopped me; and I think I could do it again.

URB CIV

Here, you—you, Selma—

Mr. Bertrand, uh, her name is Salma—

*What? Be quiet, you, newbie—*the sudden flick of a bead of flux, molten and dripping, he jerks back his arm just in time—*Selma, Salma, show them,* the old man offering the ancient welding wand that Salma accepts with one dexterous hand, flipping the green eye-guard down with the other, demonstrating to the class clustered behind the steel worktable how to mend a spankbot's broken arm. At the table's head the old man watches, right eye in perpetual squint, right arm clumsy to dig in his jacket pocket for what, for a contraband cigarette that Salma lights for him with a soldering gun: *Merci,* to her, then *You see?* to the rest, a brief scowl aimed his way, *see how she did? Good work! Next, we gonna fix up a dragonfly.*

And Salma nods, he nods, they all nod: two women, six men, motorbike roughriders and teenage malcontents, shaved heads and black-wrapped braids and a wispy purple beard, all the students of this cold late afternoon, but *Smoke break first,* says Mr. Bertrand, carefully checking the street before heading for the stairs, his tread heavy and uneven, like a machine on the verge of breaking down—

—*want to come?* and it takes a moment, a wasted moment, to

realize Salma is talking to him—*Me? Sure! Sure, I'll go*—then follow her down, past four grim floors of pinch locks and accordion gates, repurposed security flats, a squatters' stronghold under permanent siege, and *The Gunnysackers,* says Salma over her shoulder, *used to have, like, the whole second floor here. You heard of them, right?*

Sure. They were a rebel army, holding the heavy blast door for her to exit, into the alley with its lone bulging trash bin, out to the street's winter sun where he shivers inside his waterproof parka; Salma in her nylon anorak seems unaffected, and *Bertrand knew them,* she says, nodding toward the old man standing now at the corner, hunched and wary as a sentinel, Mr. Bertrand whose school has always been the go-to place, the place to learn how to build and burn, hack a sex toy, defy the government. *Bertrand knows everybody. Ask him sometime about his friend the poet, the one who broke off a citizen cuff—*

Broke a cuff? That couldn't have happened.

It did happen. Lightstick fished from a kangaroo pocket, she offers him a cigarette, he shakes his head; blowing smoke, her throat is smooth and brown as buckwheat honey. *He broke it off and got away.*

The citizen cuffs were unbreakable—

They say dragonflies are unbreakable, too, white smile around the yellowed cigarette, but *Material flaw,* he says firmly. *The dragonfly design is flawless, only the material can fail—*

You're sticking up for a dragonfly? one eye screwed shut, right eye, like Bertrand's—and then she smiles again, a joking smile because it must be a joke, who would stick up for dragonflies, and the police state that launches them, their lasers and tasers, and *Flawless design,* he says, with a smile of his own, half a feint, half at that skin, those hazel eyes below the fireproof bandana, Salma like a princess in welder's drag. *You have to give credit where credit's due.*

Is that how they do it uptown?

Uptown? No, no actually I'm from Montréal—

Canada? they still have that? another joke, waiting for his smile in return, then *Montréal,* she says, *that's a long way away. How'd you wind up here?* as a cough booms, Mr. Bertrand's ugly and wet, no wonder cigarettes are illegal! but Salma drags deep, waiting for his answer, so *I came from school,* he says. *My master's in Urb Civ—placement derangement, but it's really about how things work together. Or fall apart—*

You mean like this, her backhand gesture to the building, the scorched and boarded block: a storefront mosque and silent tavern, old transit shelter grayed out by years of vandalism, sharp piss smell even in this cold. *My degree's in folklore studies . . . I bet your profs never saw anything like this in real life.*

You bet right, which is exactly why he came here, why he volunteered for active service—call it spying, call it infiltration, without boots on the ground nothing will ever change. And this place, this city, is overdue for change, for rescue, black rings of decay around all the world's cities like a fable of rot and danger, the dark forest strangling the fair castle; folklore, sure. *I wanted to see if I could help, so instead of wasting time in grad school, I came here.*

Do you like it here?

What do you mean? and when she does not answer, *It's a great city in some ways,* thinking of where he stays, the quiet dormlike apartment uptown: there are other agents in the building, he knows, though none of them know each other or each other's names, even at university they never knew each other's names. In his neighborhood the sidewalks are busy and the trains are mainly clean, the tea kiosks on the corners are clean, the signs and billboards advertise products that, on this street, a person would be jumped or worse for even having. *It's better than where I came from*—not Montréal after all but New Miami, where the security still depends on drones, slow and clunky as an old man stumping downstairs: nothing like these dragonflies, fast and accurate, nearly silent, once you hear it, it's already deployed . . . The first time he saw one here he nearly gasped: that something so useful and lethal could be so beautiful, too.

You ever been to Pumptown? That's where I live.

By the, the water treatment plants—People live there? You live there?

A lot of us do, nodding toward the building, *Jorge does, and his sister . . . It's kind of rough, but at least you can drink the water, right? And the river's right there, you get a nice breeze on warm nights—it's pretty.*

Pretty? with such flat disbelief that she laughs, and *The old sodium lights,* she says, *they shine orange, like a harvest moon. And when the sharks come out—*

Sharks—

The kayakers, sketching a shape in the air, *strange beast, a bullet with fins. They race bank to bank, like shadows, they go so fast—*

Isn't that prohibited? To be on the water?

Prohibited? Yeah. This, flicking ash, *is prohibited too. So is Bertrand, so are we,* and she gives him a gentle push, nudge, shoulder to shoulder, so close he can smell her, past the cigarette stink her skin is like soap and flowers, and *How did you know my name?* with a different kind of smile, and *I asked that one kid, with the beard,* looking at her then away, as if clumsy, abashed, but *You,* she says, *could have asked me.*

He says nothing, formulating the best answer, best response—because Salma is why he came here, to befriend her, learn what he can from her, all the tactics and plans; and turn her if he can, turn her the right way, and her friends with her, the kid with the beard, Jorge, who is Jorge—and *A folklore degree,* he says at last, bantering, nudging back. *What can you do with a folklore degree?* to bring her shrug: *"All learning comes to use," that's what my professor used to say. And folklore is history, right, it's based in—*

History? History's over, it's dead. This is what's real, recalling with scorn his own professors' toothless classroom philosophies, their fantasies of block-by-block reclamation, gentrification, like posh blinds on smashed windows, their dither and dismay at the steep rise in state security, the surrender of personal freedom—but what if they saw this city up close? *Freedom!* like illegal kayaks racing in filthy water, dirty waste canisters rolling loose at the curbs, in the subway—on his way here today, on the train, he sat reading or trying to read as a man in a hat with plastic bull's horns slumped next to him, squirming and panting, masturbating? having a seizure? but no security available, no one there to make it stop: so he got off at the next stop but the next train was nowhere, the arrival display pulsing and falsing, unreadable runes, so he headed for the stairs, as sounds assailed him from the shadows, sly and sourceless, something like footsteps but not footsteps, three-legged, what walks like that? and who on the platform to ask for help? No transit police, no buzzbox to push, nothing to do but shine his phone in the direction of the sounds, and *I can see you*, he called, loud, lying, voice too high, *I'm recording you!* And be answered with nothing but a mocking silence, a metallic chuckle that turned out to be another canister, waste canister, rolling drunkenly toward him, to fall with a hollow *thunk* on the tracks, an invisible hazard to any oncoming train—and he hurrying up to the street again, to the breakage and emptiness, the roaming trashhawks with their sagging sacks and sharp sticks, the trucker-fuckers who flash themselves to any passing vehicle, down to this building where the blast door wears an ugly red glyph that means, who knows what it means? folklore, some sign from history, here be monsters? Does Salma understand what this school, this "learning," is *about*?

And what if he took her to his building, his quiet street lined by containment walls, firm blue blast-resistant concrete, and the clean new public park with its smart pickets, that waist-high white fencing that self-multiplies as needed, put down three and in an hour there are thirty, or three hundred, a thousand, some people call them dragon's teeth; folklore again. And the dragonflies, what would folklore call them? everything but what they are, eyes to see and power to patrol, control, punish if need be, every legal citizen in this city should have one, like sleepless guardian angels: because in real live actual life, bad things happen that need to be punished, cities rot and die if they are not properly policed, professors are idiots and agents are recruited and rebels are removed so that one day cities, all the cities, this city, can be safe again, can be a place to live and not a place to fear, here be monsters—

—*even in folklore. No one's exempt, the heroes, the villains*—she is talking, what is she saying, something about good and evil, some romantic's fable, the anorak's hood framing her face, princess in the gutter—then *Hey,* she says, voice changing, one hand on his arm. *Are you OK?*

I'm fine. He realizes he is shivering, a quick hard shudder, another. *It's just, it's cold out here,* cold enough, now, to snow, fresh spinning flakes from the clustering clouds, and upstairs will be nearly as cold, no real heat in this building or Mr. Bertrand's rooms—

—as here comes Mr. Bertrand, crippled and slow, not long for this world, yet how much harm has he already done, how many have been trained in his lawless school with its Gunnysacker pedigree, its stolen tools and siphoned power, corrupting people like Salma who set out to do good? But no one is exempt from law, yes, or force, take a hex head screwdriver, and pop! goes an eye, the other eye, how many students can a blind man teach? If it were up to him—

And *You trying to school him, too, this blockhead?* Mr. Bertrand gruff to Salma, and then to him, *The women are smarter, always, that's why there's five boys here for every girl. You keep watching, you'll learn . . . Inside, inside now*—

—as Salma holds the blast door, this time, for him, following close, companionably close, close enough to abruptly pivot then press him to the stairwell, her forearm hard against his throat, and *Did you think,* she says, her voice changing again, her face changing with it, like a mask removed, *we didn't know about you? Did you think we didn't see you coming?*

What—Wait, Salma, I don't—

Canada my ass—

Salma no—as that strong arm presses, and presses, as he struggles against her, struggles for air, for freedom, as Mr. Bertrand holds the blast door closed, Mr. Bertrand who knows everybody, Mr. Bertrand watching as his eyes roll up and his knees give way, Salma's arm harder still, like iron, like a machine, her face without expression, beautiful useful le

—for Carter Scholz

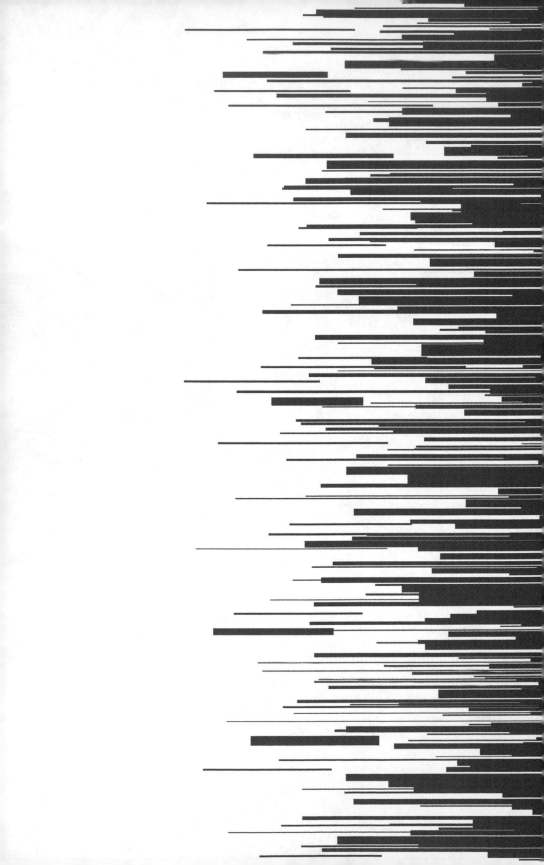

ON THE WAY

FIREFLIES

Look, he said. *Look at all the stars.*

Steep back steps, less porch than stoop, rusting wrought iron railing and barely room enough for two, but they had once been lovers, and so it was easy to sit touching, hip to thigh. His head back against the screen door mesh, looking up; on her right arm a fresh bandage, white and still, like a large moth waiting with folded wings.

They look like fireflies, she said. Awkward, left-handed, she lit a cigarette; without being asked, the man opened her bottle of beer, an Egyptian beer called Stella, *star.* He had just come back from Cairo; she was going somewhere else.

Fireflies? he said. He had a kind of accent, not foreign but not native either: unplaceable long vowels, sentences that curled up at the ends, like genie's slippers, like the way they talk down south. *One big backyard, to have fireflies that size?*

Think of the grasshoppers, she said, and laughed, winced, dragged on her cigarette. The smoke rose in the darkness; it was very late. *Or the dragonflies.*

Or the June bugs, he said. His own beer was almost empty. *What'd the doctor say?*

She did not answer. The cement of the steps was damp, clammy against the backs of their legs; like a slab, a tomb, tombstone, and *Esperson called,* she said. *He told me they were taking my paper.*

The, the vacuum one? Oh honey that's great! He pressed her leg, the bare skin below the edge of her cutoffs; his hand was warm, with long strong workman's fingers, small hard spots like rivets on the palm, his skin a topographic map of his days: cut wood, carry water, name and number and know all the plants in the world. Sometimes she imagined him out there in the green aether of the woods, any woods: mending a split sapling, digging arbutus, testing the soil. He the earth, she the void, and *When does it come out?* he asked. *When will you—*

When do you leave again? she asked. *Where are you going?*

Montreal, he said, *but not till December? or maybe the new year, I'm not sure. It depends on— It depends. When did Esperson say—*

Look, she said, one hand out, her left hand with its tubed coal of cigarette. *Fireflies; look.* Above the dark drenched grass a ballet of on and off, little lights delicate, sturdy, irregular. From the porch, they watched together in silence, a long wondering silence; he put his hand on her leg again, and squeezed, but absently; he sees this all the time, she thought. In the woods.

Your paper, he said. *Tell me what it's about. In layman's terms?*

Shifting a little on the steps, trying not to move her right arm, and *Basically,* she said, *it's about how most of what's out there, most of what's here—*tapping her chest—*is vacuum energy. The cosmos is one-third visible and dark matter, two-thirds vacuum energy.*

He flicked away an insect, a mosquito, some tiny night-borne pest. *I thought nature abhors a vacuum?*

This kind keeps the universe expanding, she said. *It resists the gravitational pull of the galaxies, and so—*

And what?

She said nothing.

What's—hey, are you OK? Are you—

She did not answer; he looked into her face, peered through the darkness then at once looked away, his own mouth twisting down one-sided, like a stroke victim's, its curve the felt echo of her pain, and *You wan' go in?* he asked, voice soft with alarm, his accent more pronounced. *You wan' lie down, or—*

No, harsh, fighting it, fighting herself; the hand with the cigarette trembled, its light like a firefly trapped in a jar until: *The doctor,* he said at last, when she had finally calmed. *He called me . . . I'm still the emergency contact, you know?*

She did not answer.

He said—

I know what he said. She took a last drag on the cigarette, let it drop and roll down the porch steps to the grass, dying red in a sea of silent green. *We had a nice long talk.*

There are things you can do. There are still things that you—

I'm not doing anything, she said. *While you were in Cairo I was doing things, and what the fuck good did any of them do me? I'm sick of all that.* She reached for the pack of cigarettes, but her grasp was unsteady, and in her lurching motion her right side, right arm, struck the black iron rail and she cried out, a brief excruciating cry; and he moaned, low and helpless, a noise unwilled as he tried to right her, but *No,* she said through her teeth, *no don't touch me, don't.*

Silence: night sounds; when her gaze had cleared, she saw that he was weeping, and *Don't,* she said, unsteady, and put her left hand on his arm, just above the elbow, the way she always had. *It's OK, it's all right*—but still he wept, face up toward the night, the wet fierce glottals of a child, until *Don't make it worse,* she said, to make him stop, and he did, slowly, sucking in his breath and *Get us another beer,* she said, to help him.

When he had gone into the house again, she laboriously lit another cigarette, sat smoking in the faint noises from inside: water running, the glass clink of bottles. The fireflies were back, as if her pain and his had scattered them like the shadow of some dark beast, but now in the beast's departure they were free again, to play, to go about their amatory errands, and *It's the males who light up,* he said, back

on the porch stoop, handing her a fresh beer. *They do it for the girls?
To get them to notice?*

It must work, she said, *or there wouldn't be fireflies.*

Wonder if it's the same up there? pointing with his own beer into
the starlit sky. *Light matter and dark matter, you said? Like blinking
on and off?*

No, she said.

*And the, the vacuum, it's what keeps them going, right? Keeps
everything going?*

Expanding, she said. *It increases the rate of expansion.*

Like this? he said, and touched not the bandage but the skin
above it, so lightly it was almost no touch at all: and she stared at
him through the dark, breath gathered in astounded and furious
hurt, but before she could speak *You're expanding,* he said, *aren't
you? Getting . . . more diffuse. Like a plant does, with seeds? Like these
trees right here, poplars—when their pods split open and all the seeds
float away everywhere? That's you. With your work, and your articles,
and, and who you are . . . It just goes on. You go on. Resisting the
pull, right? But—but like poplars out there,* pointing at the darkness.
With the big fireflies?

She said nothing. Her throat felt full and tight, like a seed pod,
ready to burst.

Big poplars, he said. *Big seeds.*

Neither spoke; her left hand took his right; their fingers linked.
Finally: *Read my paper,* she said. *When it comes out. OK? Read it
for me.*

He squeezed her hand, squeezed it slow and twice, and *Yes,* he
said, *I will. But I won't understand it.*

You understand plenty, she said.

A breeze touched the leaves of the poplars. Past them, past the
porch the fireflies moved, in the stars and the breathing night.

COYOTE PASS

I'd like to buy one of your dogs, she said.

• • •

In the empty nights she could hear them, the sharp cough of fox terriers, barking. She had never been close enough to actually see the dogs, but on her daily drive—dry cutline road from ranch to town ("town:" a post office, a diner/grocery, a dollar store and two desolate bars)—she always marked the sign: KAITLAND KENNELS, black letters above the woodcut dog, ears up, alert, alive. Woodcut—is that what that kind of thing was called? that burned-in campfire style? Her mother would have known. *Medium: fire on plywood board.* Her mother the famous art collector; every wall, dining room, living room, all three of the bedrooms, the bathroom even, stacked up in the hallway: paintings, sculpture, fabric weavings all meant for others, for no one who lived in the house.

It had taken her mother almost two full years to die; amazing, that the mind could hold on so long past the body's will to leave. Amazing too to find herself still here, the last daughter, like some figure out of a fairy tale: *While the other sisters were out dancing with the handsome princes, Last Daughter was in the castle with the queen.* Dealing with the hospice workers, the insurance company, the sound of the house at night, that nothing sound so loud she had to go outside to drown it out: into the creosote wind, the smell of sage, the darkness, the faraway barking of the dogs.

• • •

What kind of dogs are they? she asked the young woman. *Terriers?* The young woman looked not at her but pointedly over her shoulder, at the scrub, the dry mouth of the desert, the road, crushed soda cans shining like fallen jewelry. She had long black hair, a hard plastic-looking black, no highlights at all. She wore sunglasses, a T-shirt printed with fading brown Kokopellis, high-top sneakers stained red. *You want to buy one,* the young woman said, *you ought to know.*

• • •

At the post office the clerk was always sympathetic. *How's your mom doing today?* or *How's it going out there?* now that "mom" was gone and the mail had slowed to a trickle, now that there was no reason, really, for her to stay on anymore. *It must be getting lonely,* the clerk said sympathetically. He was a young man, or young-looking, anyway, why would a young man stay in a place like this, with nothing to do, nothing to see but dirt and desert and sky. Her sisters had come back twice, once for the funeral, once for the will. Carol, the oldest, had stood in the carport in her spike heels and cried: *That she lived like this, like a hermit. Poor Mother. Poor Mother!* Lindsay in the middle had shrugged, sat at the kitchen table smoking and drinking Coke. *Poor you,* she had said, grinding out one cigarette, lighting another. Smoke drifted past the empty spots on the walls where the paintings had hung, the paint beneath a different, darker color. *Anne, seriously, how can you stand this haunted house? You did what you had to do, when are you leaving?*

Soon, she had said. Her coffee was cold now, the microwave was gone. In its space on the counter was a chrome toaster oven as old as she was, resurrected from under the sink; all the old stuff, all still there. *Just as soon as everything's done.*

• • •

What's your name? the young woman asked her. Up close like this, talking, Anne could see that she was really just a girl, sixteen maybe, her cheeks rounded under the black sunglasses, her arms brown and strong. It was because she was so tall that she seemed older, tall and quiet. Watchful.

Anne Clay. What's yours?

A pickup truck shot by, Bondo and chrome in a flume of dust. Unseen, past the L-turn of the outbuildings, the battered-looking ranch house, the dogs barked on cue, as if they had been watching the road from their kennels. Watchdogs.

The girl didn't answer. Finally Anne saw that she would not. Never mind. *May I see the dogs? Or are there any puppies? I'd really rather have a puppy—*

The girl coughed, a sharp sound. *You have to make an appointment first. With my dad.*

Well, all right then, can I make—

He's not here now. The girl took off her sunglasses. Her eyes were so pale, so wintry blue, that she looked blind. White eyes, black hair, a startling combination, not attractive. *You live around here?*

I—no, not really. Well for now I do, I guess. It's my mother's house, she was an art collector, actually kind of famous: Susan Lynn Clay, maybe you've heard of her? Anyway she, she passed away, so I'm the caretaker now. And it gets so quiet out there, at night especially, I always wanted—I want a dog.

Why was she telling this to this girl who obviously did not care, this girl sliding her sunglasses back on as if to indicate that they were done talking or that she anyway was done, why was Anne saying anything at all, so *Please tell your father,* trying to sound brisk as she pushed on her own sunglasses, crooked and green, *that I want to make an appointment. I want to get a dog as soon as possible. A puppy if you have one.*

His name is Joshua, the girl said, and turned away, walking towards the outbuildings, the beige cinderblock of the kennels. Sage in the wind. On the drive back, Anne imagined herself walking a puppy, a female puppy, active, happy, alive. She would name it Sassy. It would be her dog.

• • •

Dogs shed. Dogs piddle. Dogs make a mess, Annie, I can't have a mess like that here.

But Daddy said—

I said no. No means no.

But Daddy—

Annie, stop.

• • •

There was no website, no listing with the Kennel Club, no number for Kaitland Kennels, but the young post office clerk was helpful as usual. Flipping through a spiral notebook as Anne leaned against the counter, next to change-of-address cards, a stack of ExMail forms, a display of neatly framed stamps. He knew Kate a little, the clerk said, he didn't think there would be any harm in sharing the number—

Kate?

Kait. She's the old man's granddaughter, Kait-Land, see? The clerk smiled. His teeth were stained a pale beige, from coffee, maybe. *It used to be called Coyote Pass, before she came. They sold some real champions, I guess, to dog show people, breeders, that kind of thing. Expensive . . . You know, if all's you want is a pup, I'd drive on up to Stovepipe. There's a Humane Society shelter there, real nice place, nice people. I got my Callie there—*

You have a dog?

A cat. Calico, "Callie," see? The clerk smiled again. *I'm allergic to dogs. Not them, but their dander, right? When they shed.* Dogs shed. Dogs piddle. Dogs bark. The edge of the counter bit into the skin of her arms. *Want me to give you the number of the shelter in Stovepipe, too?*

I really want a terrier, she said.

• • •

She called the kennel number from the clerk: no one answered, no voicemail, nothing. She called again. And again as the sun went down, surely someone would be there by now, the girl had to come home from school, the dogs had to be fed or walked or something. And the father—or grandfather, Joshua? he had to come back sometime, didn't he?

The phone rang and rang. The wind rose, fell, rose higher again, dry words whispered from a dry throat. At ten o'clock she stopped trying and went to bed. All night she heard, she dreamed she heard, the dogs.

• • •

You prefer art to people, Susan, you always have. Why don't you just admit it?

The sound of the cigarette lighter, like something hard snapped in two. *Don't start, Ed, all right? I have to be up early.*

Annie pulls the covers up over her head, breathes through her mouth the taste of stale blanket-air. Against her chest the stiff warmth of the stuffed poodle, white fur, red plastic collar. Kids at school say their parents fight, too, scream and yell at each other, swear. Bobby Reddings said his mother once threw a whole plate of food at his dad, mashed potatoes and gravy, it ran down the wall and then they both laughed. Annie knows that this kind of fighting is different.

No one is going to laugh after this. She hugs the stuffed dog tighter, so hard she can feel its button eyes against her skin.

We have to tell the girls, her father says. *Are you going to tell the girls?*

Why don't you? her mother says. *You're the one with all the heart.*

• • •

Kait, she called, her voice a reedy echo. *Kait!*

The girl's gait never changed. If she heard Anne, or Anne's car, she gave no sign, just kept walking on the endless lunar blacktop. White jeans today, relatively clean, the same scuffed sneakers. A backpack with a graphic of the sun, cartoon yellow smile, white fangs in the curve of the smile when you got up close enough to see. By now the car was crawling, Anne's foot on the brake, and *Kait,* she said again. *Are you—do you need a ride?*

She assumed the girl would say no, expected anything, but *Sure,* Kait said, and hopped into the passenger seat as if they were old friends, as if Anne gave her a ride home every day, a ride from where? School? The air conditioning was on, a cold and necessary stream, but Kait rolled down the window, let in the baking desert air. For a minute Anne expected her to hang her head out, the way a dog would.

Are you on your way home from school?

Kait smiled, as if she were really amused; a smile like the sun's. The wind blew her hair around her face, obscuring her eyes. *You still want that puppy?*

Yes! I called, I called several times. But no one ever answered.

We've been busy, Kait said. *You want the pup, you can have him now.*

At the kennels, Anne waited outside the building, sweating in the sun; Kait did not allow her to go inside. When Kait came out, she was leading a puppy, cocked brown ears and a blunt stare; he sniffed Anne's fingertips, did not wag his tail.

Oh, what a cutie! And it's a girl? A female?
Male.
Oh. Oh he's adorable, but I really wanted a—
Only pup we have right now.
Oh.

The puppy sniffed her shoes, trotted around to sniff the back of her shoes, sat down to scratch vigorously at his ear, and promptly fell over. Anne laughed. What difference did it make, really, if the dog was male or female? He was here, he was cute. And he was hers.

You need the papers right away? Kait said. It took Anne a moment to realize she meant the pedigree, the proof of bloodline, but *No,* she said, smiling, reaching to pick up the puppy. He eluded her, darting sideways; she tried again. Finally Kait snatched the puppy by his scruff and handed him, wriggling, to Anne.

What about—the puppy struggled in her arms. *I need to pay—*

When you get the papers, Kait said. *You got a leash?* When Anne shook her head, Kait disappeared into the kennel building, returning with a mostly threadbare blue cord. *He'll bust that,* she said, looping it lightly around his neck. *Don't leave him tied out with it.*

I'm not going to put him outside, for goodness sake. He'll sleep in the house, with me.

• • •

But he did not sleep. Eat, yes, even though she had no Puppy Chow—no food, no leash, she had not been prepared, Kait had utterly surprised her—but he ate the ground beef from the canned chili, then promptly crapped on the kitchen floor. Housebreaking, of course she would have to train him to go outside, but not with a leash like that, he'll bust it, yes, run into the desert, and then what? Anything could happen out there, there were wild animals, coyotes every night.

She tried to play with him, but he was more interested in investigating the house, every room, every corner, he peed a couple of times then finally curled up on the bathmat, eyes open, watching her as she fussed over a bowl of water, some cereal and milk, did dogs like milk? or was that just cats? If she had had a pet in childhood, she would have known these things. *Do you like milk?* she asked the puppy. *What should I name you?* Sassy was a girl's name. Maybe Spike. *Is your name Spike?* The puppy stared at her.

Finally she went to bed, closing the bathroom door tightly behind: not good to let him wander, his first night in a strange house. She resolved to sleep lightly, so she could hear him, deciding that if he whined she would take him into her bed. Not a good precedent to set, maybe, but still, if he was crying, if he was lonely . . .

The first time, it jolted her awake, the terrible painful keening noise, *Oh my God she's dying!* as she stumbled down the hall, two thoughts at once—*No she's already dead* and *It's the puppy*—to turn her from the old, empty bedroom to the bathroom, hand on the knob, the puppy inside not harmed in any way, or any way that she could see, just sitting there on the bathmat screaming his head off. When she squatted down, hands shaking—*What's the matter, what's wrong?*—he quieted, and edged away from her, off the bathmat onto the floor. He drank some water. He resumed his seat on the mat. She tried to pet him, but he edged away again. Finally she clicked off the overhead light, clicked on the nightlight, slowly closed the door.

She had not even fallen back to sleep before he started screaming again; it was amazing that something so small could create such a huge sound. She tried everything she could think of: petting him, turning the fan on and off, leaving the lights on, scraping more chili beef into a bowl. Nothing stopped him. He was relentless.

Finally she went outside, coat wrapped tight over her nightgown no match for the cold, the dark, the echo of his cries amplified—was it? Or was it, yes, the dogs from the kennel, of course! It had to be, he had to hear them, was screaming for them. For his mother . . . Eventually the cold became more unbearable than the noise; she turned reluctantly inside.

When at last he stopped, abruptly, like a slammed door, she lifted the pillow from her head, eyes dry and wide. Already it was getting light, a little, that faint white diffusion of earliest dawn. She thought, *It's too late now, I won't sleep,* but immediately she did.

• • •

When she woke, late, almost eleven o'clock, the first thing she did was check on the puppy. The bathroom was empty. Bowl, bathmat, a fresh puddle of pee behind the toilet, but no puppy. No puppy? Where in God's name—? She checked the AC vent, but it was intact, bolted to the wall. The window was too high and did not open anyway. There was no way the puppy could have escaped. But he was gone.

The only other way—had she left the door open, somehow? careless in her sleepless state, and he escaped into the house somewhere? or even outside? I'm not going to let him outside, for goodness sake, but had she? Had he somehow gotten out, into the yard, the desert, and—The coyotes, or a hunting cat might kill a puppy. She walked all the way to the road and back, squinting in the sun, calling *Spike! Spike!* At last she sat on a rock and cried. It was no use, he didn't know Spike was his name, didn't know her, would not come to her voice . . . Then she remembered the kennels, the all-night barking of the dogs.

• • •

Outside there were two trucks, a black pickup so shiny it looked lacquered, and a crusty maroon SUV. Anne pulled behind the pickup, turned off the ignition, sat as the air conditioning faded and the car grew warm, then hot. On the seat beside her was a brand-new red leash and a red harness sized for a puppy. She left them there and headed for the kennels.

Spotless cages, clean gleaming steel, sixteen cages and six adult dogs, no sign of the puppy. None of the dogs barked when she entered, but they all looked at her, bright black eyes, white-muff muzzles, toast-colored ears cocked to her footsteps.

Kait? she called into that quiet, and like a cannon, like a row of cannons, the dogs began to bark, hoarsely, furiously, chest-deep booms to turn her on her heel, send her scurrying back outside like a felon—

Hey there, wait! Hey!

A man, older man in filthy jeans and a stained T-shirt, KAIT-LAND KENNELS in black, the woodcut campfire dog. White hair, no smile. *Who're you? Why you botherin' my dogs?*

I'm looking for Kait, she said, breathless. *I was here yesterday, and she— The puppy—*

What puppy?

The puppy she gave me. He's missing, he—

What puppy? he said again as another man appeared, baggy shorts and a red tank top, leading a puppy on a frayed blue leash, and *That's him!* she cried, dropping to her knees to reach for the puppy who wiggled joyfully under her touch, wagging his tiny tail. *Oh thank God, I thought he was lost, I— He must have heard the dogs, he must have come back to find his mother—*

Both the men looked at her, then at each other. *Ma'am,* the man in the tank top said, *I'm not sure what you mean. This is my dog.*

No, no, he's mine, I brought him home yesterday. Her voice sounded high and tinny with relief, like helium. The pup's fur was soft and plush under her fingers. *But he ran away.*

The men looked at each other again, the white-haired man shook his head. *You're mistaken.*

No, you don't understand! Ask Kait. She gave him to me, she even gave me that leash—

You go on, the older man said, and the tank top man said, *Thanks, Josh,* and bent to scoop the puppy away, Anne reaching for him, crying, *No, no, ask Kait, she'll tell you!* Until *Missus,* the older man said, sharp, *I don't know what kind of game you're playin' here but unless you got papers or a receipt you better—*

But Kait—

—take it down the road.

The tank top man tucked the puppy close to his chest, opened the pickup door. *Come on, Sass,* he said, quietly. *Good girl, come on.*

Why are you doing this to me? Anne asked the man, expecting no answer; already she felt tears in her throat, tears of defeat, already she was turning back to her car, hot and unbearable, the little leash and harness on the seat. The dogs starting barking, six dogs sounding like sixty, watchdogs, as she flung the car into reverse and almost hit the SUV, flung it into drive—

—and there in the kennel doorway, sunglasses and red sneakers, hair in a black braid, was Kait: grinning, was she grinning? or just showing her teeth? As *Kait!* Anne cried, and slammed the brakes so hard the airbag popped, punching her back in her seat; when she finally struggled free of the car, the girl had gone.

• • •

All set? the mail clerk asked, smiling his sympathetic beige smile. *Got everything you need?*

Yes, Anne said. *Thank you.* From outside the impatient horn, Anne's car but Lindsay drove it as if it were a rental. She had picked it up from the dealership in Stovepipe, towed there from the kennels, Anne weeping as she called AAA; the white-haired man had refused to speak to her, or even to let her wait inside, out of the sun. Kait never reappeared.

Oh hey, the mail clerk said. *I been meaning to ask, did you ever get that dog? From Kaitland Kennels?*

Yes, Anne said. Her chest still ached from the airbag, a hard, hollow feeling. *But she—she died.*

Oh that's a shame! I'm so sorry. Anne said nothing, staring at the counter, at her hands on the counter. Finally, *Well have a good trip, then, anyway,* the mail clerk said. *Take care.*

Thank you, she said again, knowing it was not a trip, knowing she would not be back. *You too.*

In the car Lindsay clicked the radio up a notch, some howling

Tex-Mex harmony; the air swam with smoke. She tapped the green triangle hanging from the rearview mirror—tree-shaped air-freshener, fake pine reek—and *Christ,* Lindsay said, *the whole car smells like dog, they'll have to power-clean it before they can sell it. Anyway you won't get much. No offense, but you look kind of terrible, Annie. What's been happening in that mausoleum, anyway?*

Anne put on her sunglasses, new sunglasses, desert brown. *Nothing,* she said. On the way to the airport they had to pass Kaitland Kennels. The radio was much too loud for her to hear any barking. The campfire dog, she noticed, stared straight ahead at the road.

ROAD TRIP

"Look for a storefront," the woman in the gas station tells you. Older woman, older than you anyway, yellow GO GATORS! T-shirt, skinny elbows planted on the counter and "Oaktree and Madison, it's in a little strip mall, next to a Cigarette King. Says BCI on the window, but the louver-blinds are always shut." Lights then puffs on her own cigarette, cigarette queen smiling at you through the smoke. She's not going to say anything else, so there's nothing to do but go back into daylight, strong sunlight and the heat of the car's front seat, it's cooking like an oven and it isn't even noon. How can people live in a climate like this? Why did you even come?

Okay. In a strip mall, Okay. Pass a drugstore, discount store, various restaurants (The Oasis, Redd Robbin's), the Home Improvement Barn; trolling and craning through the traffic and the heat, through the secret crawl of sweat on your back, sour elixir of salt and light. The thickets of skepticism, the forests of desire, *oh sure,* as you trawl down Madison, looking for Oaktree, looking for a strip mall and BCI on the window, *the louver-blinds are always shut,* what for? So no one can see what they do in there? So no one can see you, doing what no rational person would or should do, committing the cardinal sin of stupidity and need? *Gonna wade in the Jordan, wade in the Jordan, let the waters break over my head—*

—and there it is, Cigarette King, way over on the opposite side of the road so you have to pass it to turn around, *pass it and keep going*, your mind advises, the part that still can reason, the part ungripped by pain: the pain that never passes, that never wavers or abates, that wakes you dry-eyed in the night until you have to get out of bed and walk, walk, walk it down—because you can't drink it down, not anymore, right? Even when you get out of rehab? Even when they give you back your car?

Where are we going?

Nowhere, baby. Just for a ride.

—and the dog in the back seat, don't forget the dog, tail wagging and—

There's a parking space right by the door, left just for you. The letters on the window are plain and nondescript, BCI, Before Christ Incorporated, Bullshit Created Inside, it can mean whatever you want it to mean, it can be whatever you need it to be, isn't that what that woman had said? The herbalist, spiritualist, whatever the hell she was, she was Elizabeth's idea but you were the one she spoke to: *They'll be able to help you*, her hand warm on your arm, was she coming on to you or what? with Elizabeth right there, Elizabeth who could hardly bear to look at you, Elizabeth who was turning to stone right before your very eyes, so *All right*, you said, because there was nothing else you could say, nothing else to do but buy the goddamned plane ticket, take the time off from work and *What will you tell them?* in the bed, in the morning, her face turned like a bas-relief towards the window, gray skies and weeping rain. *At work, I mean? How will you get the time off to—*

I already told them, you said, a lie meant to soothe her, the whole thing was meant to soothe her, wasn't it? make her look at you, come back to you again? because without her there was nothing left and no one, nothing living but the pain, and so you lied and left, just another in a chain of lies laundered by noble intent, like sticking drug money in the poorbox, does that make it better? does it even matter? And why are you sitting out here like this, in the car, in the sun, in the fist of the heat? Are you stalling? Are you frightened? Of what?

They'll be able to help you, they who? but the spiritualist-herbalist had been less than precise about that: a healing group, she had called them, without specifying exactly what was done to whom and how this healing might be accomplished. Maybe just getting on the plane had done it, maybe you could turn around and go home right now, tell Elizabeth another lie, she must be used to them by now, right? *It was wonderful, honey, I went right into the light*—no, that's what you do when you're dead, right?

Where are we going?

Nowhere, baby. Just for a ride.

Two women come out of the cigarette store, glance at you, keep walking: will they go into BCI, too? but instead they step into the dry cleaner's, come out carrying suits, men's suits dark in swathing plastic, suitable for funerals; Elizabeth wore white. Mass of the Angels. Who even believes this shit? Her? You? Anybody? Are you going to sit here all day?

Go in. Go on.

Air conditioning, a dry refrigerator smell; for a moment you just breathe in, cool air like a circulating gas, like anesthetic. Not a big space, but adequate: folding chairs stacked on a dolly, a card table with a phone and a CD player, posters on the walls, anonymous sunsets and waterfalls, nothing overtly religious, thank God and—

"Hello," a woman's voice, it makes you jump: she sees, she smiles and "Hello," again; she's young, twenties maybe, slim and blonde, that pure white-blonde like Elizabeth, like—"Are you here for the service?"

Yes.

"You're a little early," kindly, "but that's fine. Would you like to read some of our literature while you wait?"

No; but you do, a hand stuck out automatically like on the street, flyers for this or that, save twenty percent, save the whales, save yourself, and the "literature" she gives you is as bland as the posters, just a lot of low-key new-ageish crap about the soul, restoring the soul, it could be an advertisement for a facelift or a spa . . . so maybe this won't be so bad, you think, sitting back in the folding chair, maybe this won't be much of anything and you can get right back in the rental car and head for the airport, maybe even get home tonight, home to lie beside Elizabeth and—

"Sir? Could you—" from the blonde, smiling, struggling with the dolly's release and Here, you say, hands atop hers on the catch, her hands are so small. Here, let me.

As you help her free the chairs a small tone sounds—*ping!*—a digital doorbell and here come two more supplicants: a man your age and a very old woman, oxygen tether and terrible bright eyes; she gives you the once-over as you stand there with the blonde, and "Well hello," the blonde says, "how are you?" as you keep setting out chairs, joined now by the old woman's caretaker? son? until thirty chairs are lined in three neat rows.

And all the while the door keeps pinging, people keep coming in, why so many people in the middle of a workday? Mostly women, mostly middle-aged but there are a few young ones, and even, most dreadfully, a couple of kids, a boy and a girl, but fortunately they're both dark and fat and sullen, they sit kicking the backs of the chairs and each other as their mother? no, grandmother, keeps hissing at them to hush.

"She started it, she—"

"You hush!"

And then the music begins, tinkling windchime piano, and "We welcome you all here," says the blonde, in a louder, more professional voice. "We're so glad you can be with us today. We're going to start with a song, 'Love is the Light We Follow'" and off they go, most of them seem to know the words; is this a radio-type song or church or what? You don't sing, of course, you listen, listen because you can't help it, because it keeps your mind off what you came here to do—

—which is what? Ask forgiveness? weep healing tears? dump all your guilt like a steaming load of shit and float away redeemed? *I wish I was dead,* you said a hundred times to Elizabeth, said it as she held you and cried, said it until *I wish you were too,* with her hand over her eyes, mouth drawn down like a stroke victim's; after that you never said it again but *How do you think it is for me?* you wanted to say, walking the floor with the pain, monster baby no one else could see, *how'd you like to be in my shoes* with nothing but memory for companion, nothing but the sun and the non-smell of vodka, the dog in the back seat wagging his tail, she wriggling in the booster seat because its straps were bugging her, making her fuss and whine so, *You can be a big girl,* you said, remember? *Be a big girl up front with the seatbelt*—which of course she loved, up front with Daddy, with the non-smell of vodka, with the dog in the back—

barking and barking

crying

—and the scatter of bottle glass gleaming in the sun, bottle glass and safety glass and your teeth—remember?—your own teeth mixed up with the glass, and you were sorting through it, somehow thinking if you could find your teeth everything would be all right—

—as "Love is the light we follow / Love is the dream we need / Love is the new tomorrow / Love is the flowering seed"—jesus who writes this crap? and look at them all singing along like it was Mozart, what are they here for anyway? And the laugh rises in your chest, black metastasizing laugh, because what would they do if you started shouting, calling it out like some mad MC, anybody here with cancer? How about MS? emphysema? leukemia? AIDS? What's the matter with you, little girl, little dark girl with the big fat stomach, is it you or your brother or your grandma who needs help?

"Let's pray," and it's a new voice, a woman's voice: sweet as honey and soft as smoke, a voice so compelling you crane your head to see her face: but she's nondescript, fortyish, in oversized glasses, brown pageboy and brown blouse, with her mouth shut you'd never notice her at all.

But "Let's pray," with such seductive power, such insistence that you let the woman on your right, one of the younger ones, take your hand as you reach for the person on your left, the man with the oxy-gen-mother, it feels strange to hold a man's hand. The minister held your hand, remember? until you told him to stop, took your hand away, hugged it against your body as Elizabeth moaned—

don't touch me don't touch me—

"We ask for healing. We ask for solace. We ask for what is broken to be made whole," says the woman with the voice, an incredibly sexy voice if you don't look at the dumpy face, what would it be like to make love to a voice like that? and "We ask for healing," the woman says again, so close now you start, is she talking to you? No, to the oxygen-woman, those bright bird-eyes closing as the woman takes her hands, bird-claw, liver-spotted hands, strokes and kisses them, ugh—but the old woman is crying, and the son is crying and "Be healed, Virginia," the woman with the voice says, the words one long caress; how does she know her name? Are they repeat visitors, regulars? and does that mean whatever this is doesn't work, you have to keep coming back? *You're* not coming back. "You want to be healed, don't you?"

Simple as that, huh? as the old woman weeps, and coughs, the oxygen line trembling like a scuba diver's, going deeper and deeper, but for you the disappointment is like a gust of clean air, is that all this is going to be? Just like watching a TV evangelist, just a lot of blow-dried histrionics, but what else did you expect? She'll come to you next, take your hand, murmur some crap in that sexy voice and then you can—

—but she passes you entirely, heads for the grandma and the kids, ah Christ it would have to be the kids, and "Praise Jesus," says the grandma; if you turn your head a little—and you do—you can see her tears, too, long clear lines on that round, dark face. "Make him whole."

"What's the matter with you, Shawn?" the woman asks the boy; and now that voice is a mother's, a sweet teacher's, the teacher you most want to please, and "I got asthma," says the boy, his gaze all trust, his hand in hers. "I can't breathe good when I play."

"What do you like to play?" as the song on the CD changes, something about going home, *when I go home,* and "Soccer," says the boy. "Soccer and—"

"Basketball," the girl breaks in, not to be left out; she takes the woman's other hand. "He don't play very good, though. *I* always—"

"Be healed, Shawn. You want to be healed, don't you?"

"Yes," says the boy—and then screams, just like that, screams and bucks like he's just been shot, and the grandmother cries out as if she felt the bullet too—and you jerk away from all of it, stumbling into the son next to you who stares at you like *What's your problem?* as the boy shrieks again, a teakettle cry that sinks to a wheeze then becomes a whimper; but now he's smiling, the grandmother is smiling, the girl stares avidly at them both, and "Better," says the woman with the voice; it's not at all a question; she knows. "Better now."

And then it's onto the next one, and the next and the next: younger woman touching her breast, older woman with crippled hands, an old man with "cancer liver," he says, with a deaf man's flat high volume, "I got cancer liver," and "You want to be healed?" she asks them all, as if she's checking it out with them first, making sure, sharp salesperson bringing the mark in on the sale, which is what you want to think, what you do think—except for that smell in the air, a definite smell like thunderstorms, ozone, except for the little boy, Shawn, whose eyes are glowing, he keeps taking deep breaths and letting them out, in and out, and two steps from you the old lady with the oxygen tether has slipped it from her nose, a woman in a faded blue tube top is saying, "I can feel it! I can feel it!" to the fat friend beside her who's clutching her arm; everything stinks of ozone and there's sweat on the back of your neck, sweat though the room is chilly, sweat though you don't believe because this is not real, this is not *real,* who does she think she is anyway? Billy Graham? Jesus Christ? because some things just can't be healed, no matter what she says in that seductress voice, no matter what you or Elizabeth or anyone else may want or long or pray for: because time runs only forward, life runs into death and stops, stops like a brick wall crumbling from the impact, stops like a body flung into the air—

—like a circus trick like black magic you watched her go fly hurled free by velocity right through the windshield why didn't the airbag work? yours worked you lived she flew: bright hair black blood there in the street like the worst thing you'd ever seen it was the worst thing and the dog too jesus christ that your dog sir? and you scrabbling through glass for your teeth head spinning mouth a dark wet flap of blood and Oh no you said just like that, the simple round vowels of a clown, a liar, a killer, oh no in simple dismay because time had not stopped when your car had and now she was dead dead forever and you were drunk and alive—

alive, oh

oh no

Where are we going?

Nowhere, baby

—because being alive means you have to live, hospital, police station, lawyer's office, home—and home become worse than a prison, prison would be a relief, no Elizabeth there with her swollen eyes and ice-cold hands, and *Why?* she asked you once, just once, everything there in that one word, and of course you had no answer, what answer was there?

Because I was drunk. Because she was whining. Because I didn't think anything bad would happen.

Because I wanted to.

"You want to be healed, don't you?" and she's back in your row now, working her way down, hands on a massive woman in a hideous off-white blouse, she looks like a weather balloon, and she's mumbling and spitting as the music changes again, going not home but up this time, *going up we're going up,* we're flying, baby, whee! "Sandra, tell me, do you want to be healed?"

"Yes," like a groaning organ, player piano running down, eyes squeezed shut, and in a few minutes it'll be over, all over and you can go, *go into the light* and the heat and the rental car, back home to nothing, nothing—

—and now she's in front of you, voice and bad glasses and all: and her eyes through those glasses are not what you expected, not professionally kind, not measuring or shrewd but something else, something you don't like but can't name, well she can't name you either can she? but "You're in a lot of pain, aren't you?" and she not only knows your name but your nickname, the name everyone calls you, she calls you that now as she keeps gazing at you with those eyes, that look you can't bear, you're sweating like a pig and all you want to do is run away but—

"You want to be healed, don't you?"

—in that voice like a lover's, staring at you in the ozone chill, staring at you like Elizabeth and the cop and the judge . . . and Caitlin, Caitlin Caitlin Caitlin flying through the air, fairy princess, baby gumdrop squashed flat as a bug and—

You want to be healed don't you?

Don't you?

—with her hands out and reaching: waiting in the white room of your terror, the palace of your guilt; waiting for you to make a move, to say Yes, I do. I do.

• • •

Don't you?

• • •

The smell of ozone in your mouth: the flung glass glittering like ice.

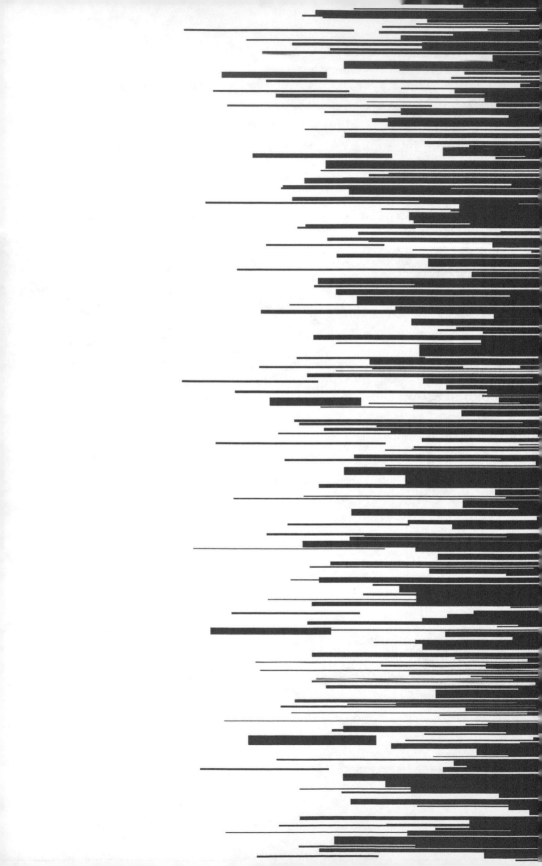

OVER THERE

TOUJOURS

Hey, hey, is he in? That's how they talk to me, these girls, girls with their knee boots and tiny little telephones, leaning against the elevator doors, tugging on their hair, lighting cigarettes—cigarettes! and right on the building wall the sign NO SMOKING. In Italian *and* English! *Hey, is he in?*

Foolish, I told my wife, my Lu. *These girls—twenty years I am with Señor, and not one of these girls will ever learn my name.*

She shrugged; she poured the coffee. Her hair, in the sun through the windows—gold and silver, like a painting, a Titian. *Ah,* she said, *they are infants. Can you be angry with an infant? Besides, Carlos knows your name . . . Maritsa called again this morning. The christening dinner—*

Señor may need me. Today the journalists come, and the man from the art school—I will try.

To give the toast, at least? He is your grandson. And Maritsa says—

I took her hand, her left hand with that tiny seed-drop of a diamond; she deserves something grander, I have said this before. *I will try.*

And then I was on my way, from the table, the apartment with the sunny windows, the terrace where she grows her flowers, pots of white daisies, I used to call her "Daisy," as if she were an

American girl. The smell of French coffee in the hallways, the stone faces at each landing like the saints and gargoyles one sees at cemeteries: weighing, approving, denying— That journalist, that English fellow from *Le Pop!* said the same last month of me: *An aging but formidable factotum, forever looming like a gargoyle over the Ezterhas brand*: that is how this business is, if there is nothing to say, still they must say something. This business, where the money flies and they take so many drugs, and the girls—"infants," yes, and younger all the time, but none too young to spread themselves for anyone, anywhere, at the shows, in the atelier, the things I have seen—!

See them now, this very morning in Gold Street: one busy with her little phone, the other scowling behind round black sunglasses, the Desmundo glasses they all wear this season, leaping up like greyhounds when I approach: "Listen, hey *listen*, Carlos wants me, he called—" while the other one shoves forward, "Me too—he wants me too!" Breathless and rude all the way up in the elevator, but I make them wait outside, Señor inside with a pair of gloves, blue leather, very nice goods. He pulls on the left, smiles at me, holds out his hand; I adjust the right.

"They sent two pair," he says, "one red and one blue. Which do you prefer?"

"Red-handed," I say, "that's guilty, *non*?" and he smiles, white as the petals of a daisy. When I first met him, he never smiled at all. "You think of everything, Gianfranco. All right, blue it is."

"Did you call for models, Señor? From Vita?" and when he nods I let them in: greedy they clamber up beside him, grab his blue hands, no thought between them to thank me who opened the door. But Señor nods as I take the empty glove case from the table, he nods and he smiles as I leave.

Later, I fish the Desmundo glasses from the pissoir. Crying, monotonous crying, from outside in the hall. The man from the art school is early, he brings another girl, another bony creature with pale hair and bright eyes, they stay for drinks, they stay for dinner. Señor has far too much wine. Maritsa sends me several angry messages. Lu is asleep when I come home.

• • •

He was half an infant himself when I met him, peasant boy with the loden jacket and the little colored pencils: serving me *café noisette*, swabbing the table, one shoulder tucked down as if something pained him: *Did you eat today?* I asked, and he shrugged, he was ashamed. Those crooked, pointed, wolfish teeth; he was ashamed of that, too, and ashamed to have been fired: *Three times in one month, from three different cafés. Because I was drawing.*

I looked at his pictures, his "girls." *You are not from the city,* I said, because already I knew him, I had been waiting for him, I knew exactly what I must do: speak to the café manager, speak to his uncle, some turd from the boroughs blustering, *He should be in school, Carlos, not making silly pictures, "fashion," what do you want with my Carlos?*

I want to feed him dinner, I said. To him I said, *Go get your things.*

For six months he slept in the room off the terrace; he helped Lu water the flowers, he went to the shops and the galleries, he drew many more "girls." When I bought the apartment on Gold Street, he worried that it was too big, too much: *All these rooms?* But *An atelier,* I said, *needs space.* The clothes followed the drawings, the first show sold all the clothes—and he came to me then, very early, still awake from the night before, and *Willys,* he said, *wants the whole line. And* Vogue *wants to interview me—she called me a wizard.* He looked around the terrace, the pots of daisies, the sun just rising. *Jesus! You're the wizard, you gave me everything, I'd still be in that fucking café if—*

Don't curse, I told him. *This was all meant to be. Consider the lilies.*

What?

Señor, I said; he almost flinched, to hear me say it. *Señor, it is my will to serve you. Always.*

• • •

Since then I have served Señor in many ways: with the journalists
and their editors; with the buyers, those sharks, and the stores, the
licensing—now they want to put his name on condoms, Ezterhas
Golden Fleece, how stupid and vulgar . . . I have served Señor as well
with the girls, the models, Señor has a sometimes regrettable taste
in models but he is always very sorry afterward, and there is always
a new girl, many new girls to choose from for a season or a night.
At times he has seemed to prefer one over another, like last winter,
that dark one from Vienna with the nervous laugh, when she went
back to Vienna Lu sighed: *Ah, Carlos, is he missing that little one?*
Why did she go, do you think?

She went because I bought the ticket, because I called her booker,
because I made it plain to her that *He deserves better*; I am wiser than
his own heart in such matters, I do not bend to heat or caprice . . .
When it is time for Señor to settle down, I will make certain that his
choice is the best one, not like the Viennese girl, or the pale thing
last night—

—who is here again, blue slacks, blue blouse, almost demure
though none of these girls ever bother with brassieres; in the sunlight
her hair is white as bone. No Desmundos for her, her gaze comes
squarely to mine as "Good morning, Gianfranco," and she hands
me a little pink bag: *amaretti* from Sofia's, the ones I most prefer, a
perfect blend of bitter and sweet. Behind me I hear Señor's approach,
rapid, the Hermès loafers he wears slapping against the marble floor.

"Gitte," he says, with far too much pleasure. "You're just in time
for breakfast."

She smiles, not at him, but to me. Her smile is very white.

"Please join us," she says.

• • •

From then on she is here every day, Gitte who smiles, who does not smoke, who speaks very little and never says where she is from, Gitte who brings *amaretti* for me until I tell her to stop, and yogurt and vitamins and machinery for Señor, today it is an ugly little steel contraption shaped like a pregnant tube: "Look," says Gitte, manipulating traps and levers until a stream of cloudy green bursts forth, sickening, a color like bile."It's a juicer," she says to my stare. "Avocado juice."

"Ah. You are a waitress, then?"

She smiles, unperturbed. Señor drinks the bile: "Oh, delicious. You cured my hangover." As he kisses her, she looks at me.

She is not a waitress, not a model, not a journalist. She came with the man from the art school, but she is not an artist, or a student: *Gitte? No,* he says when I call, *she was in the photography program but that was a while ago. I guess you could call her my assistant, kind of, she did a little bit of everything—*

A factotum.

Sure, right . . . She's amazing, isn't she? And a monster fan of Carlos, you two have a lot in common, which is true, terribly so, she knew it first but I know it now as well. The juicer, then the bracelet to count his heartbeats, then the walking trip. "Just for the weekend," Señor says to me, as if the collection is already finished, as if there is not so much work left to do, a tremendous amount of work. "Gitte says we need some fresh air." I wave one hand at the windows. "I mean—like a getaway."

"Get away from what?"

Señor does not answer. His face looks leaner, its planes more pronounced, like hers; he wears blue now as she does, his hair has been cut very short. Such great changes in such a little time, the girl has been here barely three months; it is monstrous. He fiddles with the heartbeat bracelet, he shrugs, maddening, placating: "I'll work so much better if I have a chance to relax first, Gitte knows this fantastic walking trail around Soller—"

"Spain! You don't like the sun, Señor, you have never liked—"

"—and I know—I mean, there's a little bit of friction between

Gitte and you"—he says it that way, her name first—"but if you'd only spend some time with her—You've been after me for years to slow down on my drinking, right? Now I have. She's a good influence on me, you can see that, can't you?" His voice is a plea, almost a whine. "And she respects you so much, she talks about you all the time, always asking questions—"

What sort of questions? but I do not ask because I know, the same way I know she will come to me next, and she does: dressed in blue so dark it is almost black, like the sea at night, her eyes are black as a barracuda's and "He'll work better," she says, "if he feels better. I can make him feel good . . . Why would you want to ruin that?" I do not trouble to answer. "You ought to come with us."

"To Spain?"

"To wherever we go."

I lean very close to her, so close I can smell her scent, bitter and sweet, yes: like *amaretti*, like almonds, like poison. "I have been with Señor since before you were born," I say into her ear. "I have seen girls like you come and go, many girls who—"

"There are no girls like me," she says.

We gaze at one another, there in the hallway, a phone trilling from the office, Señor whistling in the pissoir. Gitte shrugs. "If you don't come with us," she says, "you'll be left behind." And she walks away, her loafers, Hermès loafers, slapping the floor as she goes: down the hall, off to Spain, deeper and deeper into his heart.

• • •

Does one believe in lamia, in succubae? Did Medusa ever smile? What sort of perfume, one wonders, did Messalina prefer?

• • •

I sit alone on the terrace, still in my dinner jacket; Señor did not attend the Fashion Association's formal dinner, the annual dinner, everyone was there. In his stead I accepted the award, the "True Visionary" award—visionary, and he now so blind! Lu steps past the doors, calling for me, but the moon is concealed in clouds, her pots of flowers—verbena, lady's slipper—become obstacles in the darkness. She stumbles, until my hand guides her, draws her to the bench, to my side, and "Here," I say. "Sit down, I have something for you."

With my other hand I reach into my pocket for the jeweler's box, the bright canary diamond to replace the battered solitaire: I tug on her ring finger, tug until she gives a little wail, until the old ring pulls free at last. "For you, my Lu, my daisy. Take it into the light, see what I give you . . . You're not crying?"

She is crying. "Beautiful," she says. "Only—my little ring."

"You deserve better."

We sit so, I clasping her hand, she wiping at her eyes. Finally "I forgot," she says, half-rising. "You have a visitor—that nice girl, Carlos's girl," who waits for me on the landing, looking up at the gargoyles and the saints as "You come here," I say; my voice is too loud. "How dare you come here, to my home, after you kept him from the dinner, from the people who meant to honor him."

"He sent me," she says, "to tell you."

I take a step down, two steps. "Tell me what." Four steps, six. Now I am beside her, looking down at the upturned face, *forever looming like a gargoyle* and she is really very small, this Gitte, in a new blue dress—one of his dresses, already he has said he will name this collection for her, *Toujours Gitte*—small as a child, her child's hand rising, narrow fingers like twigs, if one squeezed them just a bit too hard the bones would snap in two—

"Look," she says: she wiggles her twig finger: a ring. A diamond ring. "That's where he was tonight, asking me to marry him." She smiles; she cannot help herself, foxy, satisfied, those little white teeth. "Don't you like it? I picked it out myself."

I do not answer, I cannot, my tongue feels thick and hot; the gargoyles seem to ring her, like Lilith and bad angels, her smile changes, and "Why do you hate me so much?" she murmurs. "I'm a lot like you."

"You— Where do you come from? No one knows you, no one—"

"With him I can be a queen. Like you were the king for so long. Don't worry," softly, cruelly, "there'll always be a place for you in our lives. Unless you insist on being a prick."

Now Lu is here, how did Lu come to be here? exclaiming, embracing, admiring the ring, "Why, that is wonderful, Gitte, too wonderful! Gianfranco, you knew? Of course you knew, Carlos tells you everything . . . Oh, we must have a celebration!"

"Carlos will love that," says Gitte. Her smile is fearless.

• • •

There is a celebration, a large one, everyone wants to attend, from Milan and Paris and New York; there is a wedding, even larger, even the long-ago uncle is invited. I host them both, I pay for everything, I give the toasts, I dance with the bride who wears a dress specially created by her new husband; he may design a whole new line, she says, a special collection for the modern bride. She might be a medieval queen, a Medici, in her headdress and sapphires, ice blue sapphires against her white curls; all the guests say that she looks radiant.

"You look radiant," I tell her. "You make him very happy, Señora."

"I'm glad you see that now," she says.

I give the dinner toast—"May your lives together be the stuff of dreams"—and all the tables applaud. Lu's eyes shine with tears, she kisses my cheek: "It's like being the papa, no? Though it tugs at your heart, I know it does, to have to let him go."

After dinner, he leads me aside, Señor, just past the arch of ivy and white roses: his eyes are shining, too. "What a day," he says; he wrings my hand, he is more than a little drunk. "Gitte, and you here, it's everything." He wrings my hand again. "Everything I ever wanted."

I hold him to me for a moment, just one moment; *like being the papa.* Sharper than a serpent's tooth, her white teeth: she watches from across the hall, from inside her circle of bridesmaids, of well-wishers and sycophants, she cannot hear what we say. "I wish you all happiness, Señor, always."

"I know you didn't—you weren't sure about her, at first. But I'll tell you something," he mumbles. "A secret. She's going to have a baby. A little baby boy, we saw the image at the doctor's already . . . She doesn't want me to tell anyone, but I'm telling you. Only you," and he wrings my hand again.

I draw him to me once more, I murmur in his ear. "Do this one thing for me." Radiant, yes: now I know why. A little baby boy. "One thing only. Say to me that you will name him Gianfranco."

A tear trickles down his cheek. "Jesus, sure, I will. Oh, I will."

She is leaving her magic circle, she is crossing the dance floor now. *You were the king for so long. Why do you hate me? Unless you insist on being a prick.* "Promise me, Carlos, for all I have ever done for you, for your work, all the years, everything."

"I will, I swear I will."

Now she is between us, she links her arm with his, pretends surprise at his tears, turns to me a scolding, playful look that is truly neither: "Now what's all this? Did you make my husband cry?" And she dabs with her sleeve at his eyes and laughs, and he laughs with her, and I laugh, too, just a joking old man, a funny old friend of the family, a doting grandfather . . . Half an infant when I met him, yes, but a *real* infant, a baby, baby Gianfranco, think of that. My name, my hand on the pram, my voice the first voice he hears, singing, soothing, teaching— And Mummy busy at the atelier and the office, Mummy pushing Papa along in *his* pram, why, who better than funny old grandpa to help Baby grow, to be everything his father was not, could not be, was too weak to be. Always there beside him, always my voice in his ear—

"He cries," I say, "for pure love of you, Señora." Carlos beams. She does not know how to answer me. I beam as well. "Look, they're calling you, see? Time to go and cut the wedding cake."

I shepherd them back across the floor to the cake and the

bridesmaids, I take my seat again beside my Lu, the silver knife is lifted, the happy music starts. *There'll always be a place for you in our lives,* oh my yes, Señora, *toujours.*

FAR AND WEE

My job, *senhor*, was to pull the drapes. Smooth and slow when the shows began, and quickly when they ended; sometimes very quick, the men got too excited, they wanted to climb onstage. The players laughed about it, after: *Did you see him? The walrus belly, yes, did you see? And the old one, Old Cheeseface, why I thought he would die!* They laughed as they scooped up the flowers and the calling cards, the shiny tokens stamped with a *C*. Sometimes I picked up the tokens, too, but not to keep; that would be stealing, and I am no thief.

I told him that, Master Konstantin, the first night I came, out of the snow. The last few miles, before the City, felt to me like a dream, what is it called, the very bad dream? A nightmare. I had wrapped my boots with strips of rag, my fingers were so cold they had stopped bleeding. *When did you last eat, sonny boy?* Master Konstantin asked me. *We could cast you as Rawhead and Bloody Bones . . . All these beggars. It is bad in the City, now.*

Oh no, I said. I remember I could hardly stand upright, the room— orange coals in the grate, the smell of hair oil and hot tea, the electric candles, Annelise yawning and tugging her curls—it was all like heaven to me, being inside, being warm. *I came here to work. The soldiers told me, go to the theatre. And I am strong, messire, I can work hard, I am no thief—*

That will be a nice change for us here. Annelise, call Ambrose, have him take sonny boy here belowstairs . . . Keep your hands off the players, Sonny Boy. That was the way I came to the Capitalia.

At first I did only the work no one else wanted: emptied slops, filled the grates, carried hod and water, cleaned the vomit in the jakes. The players treated me like part of the wall, sweeping on and off the stage all shiny in their costumes, their masks like the faces of birds and beasts, of demons. Some of those faces frightened me, the horns and the painted fangs, but I never showed it; I am not a child, I am a man. And some of the costumes the players wore . . .The Capitalia makes a special kind of show, you see, it is all about love, you see, between men and women. That kind of love. You understand these kinds of shows, *senhor*, I know; you live in the City.

And at the Capitalia, the players are the most beautiful of all, the most skillful in their acting; they can make anything seem real, as if it is really happening right there in front of you. This is why the men come night after night, past the soldiers, through the snow, this is why they stamp their feet and whistle and throw jewelry, and silver cigarette cases, and their calling cards, and the tokens Master Konstantin sells. Because they watch Alma, and Suzette, and Geraldina, they watch the things that they do and think, *Oh, that could be me up there, holding that beautiful lady, that could be me doing all the things that they do* . . . So the men get hot, watching. And no one made them hotter than Annelise.

It is not only that she is beautiful, *senhor*, although she is very beautiful, there is no one more beautiful at the Capitalia, in the whole City. It is the way she holds herself, the way she walks, the way she looks over her shoulder that makes you think you are the only man in the world, the only man for her. The men throw so many tokens, I have seen her wince up her eyes: "Like a hailstorm," she said, it was the first time she spoke to me, stepping off the stage, fanning herself with the feathers of her bird-mask; some of her curls were stuck to her forehead, little half-circles of gold. "Look, they hit me," turning her bare pink shoulder to show me the red marks there. "Idiots."

I did not answer her, I did not know what to say. That Annelise would speak to me! All I could do was smile, and help her gather up the tokens, dozens of tokens, we made sure to get them all. The players cash the tokens with Master Konstantin, to pay for their food and their lodging in the theatre, buy scents and silks, corn plasters for their blisters, all those things that ladies need. At first they slapped me off the tokens, but then they saw that I did not steal, so they trusted me, the ladies. Annelise trusted me.

Master Konstantin trusted me, too, more and more as the weeks went on. He put me on the door, to help Ambrose with the men; some nights he let me watch him count the money. He gave me a frock coat like his own to wear, with silver thread on the arms, and pomade to put on my hair; he showed me how to use powder to wash my teeth: "—to ease the carrion whiff. We will civilize you yet, Sonny Boy," he said, and I smiled; Ambrose frowned. Later, on the door, Ambrose said to me, "Don't mind him, that old vulture. You are civil enough already, for this place, Sonny—what was your name in your village?" but I only shrugged. I did not want to lie to Ambrose, but I did not want to talk about the village, ever, about the fields and the mud, the shit on my bare feet—I was nearly grown before I had boots to wear, the ragged boots I wore into the City, tied to my ankles with rags. I was Dusan, there, and here I am Sonny. Would Annelise let Dusan run her errands, or lace up her little shoes for her, sweet little shoes, like a child's? Would she smile at him, the way she does at me? I never want to be Dusan again.

"I am done with that," I told Ambrose, "the farm and the beasts. I am in the City now."

"Plenty beasts in the City, young man."

• • •

At first I thought he was just a drummer, one of those who go from place to place selling sundries, candies and horse tobacco, poultices for the toothache and such. Except he carried a rusty flute, and he was so dirty, he looked as if he had never been in a city before, never slept inside. His cart was dirty, too, its paint worn away, one side missing a wheel, and he pulled it himself, crookedly, like a beast. He looked like a beast, the players laughed about it: "See those woolly arms," Geraldina said. "Like a ram's. All he needs are the curly horns."

"Do you speak?" Alma asked, tugging at his coat sleeve, ragged like the rest of him. "Or can you only bray, hmm?" and she laughed, and Geraldina laughed, and Suzette, and he laughed with them; Annelise did not laugh, only sat watching and smoking, letting the smoke drift out from between her pink lips.

They all bought things from the old man—Ambrose, too; even Master Konstantin bought tobacco from "Pyotr," he said his name was, rumbling it out past his beard, the red mouth deep inside like a smelly cave, and "Don't you ever wash your teeth?" I asked him. My voice was louder than I wanted. "For the, the carrion whiff?"

"What's biting Sonny?" Geraldina asked, head to one side, smirking, Suzette giggled and I stomped away, angry; Master Konstantin asked me as well: "What ails you?" after the night's shows were over, counting out the money in his office. On his desk was the bottle of gin, he always drank while he counted. That night he offered me some. It tasted sour.

"You don't like old Drummer Pyotr and his flute, do you? That song he plays, 'Far and Wee,' it's an old song, isn't it? Ancient airs and graces . . . He's staying only for the night, tomorrow he'll be on his way. So what ails you?"

I shrugged, I did not know how to answer. No I did not like him, the way he dragged his ugly cart behind him, the devilish way he smelled. The way he looked at the ladies, at Annelise; the way she looked at him, but "He can stay or go," I said. "Either way, I don't care."

"That's the first time you've lied to me, Sonny Boy." He was smiling, counting through the coins, something was funny to him; was it me? "It's our Christian duty, is it not, to offer shelter to the vagabond and the orphan? Go on, have another drink," and I did; in the end

I drank quite a lot, enough to make me dizzy, to send me into the jakes, I thought I was going to vomit so I closed my eyes as the walls spun around me, listening to the sound of water dripping, the sound of heels click-clacking on the floor, clip-clopping like hooves—

—and I opened my eyes, *senhor*, I swear I opened my eyes and I swear I saw what I saw: that man, that Drummer Pyotr with his hairy legs ending not in shoes or boots or even feet but hooves, I swear that man had hooves like a goat's. And I looked up, straight up into his face, his laughing face beneath the shadow of the horns, and "Shall I play you a song?" he said, and his laugh was the sound the goats make when they breed. I jumped up to grab him, but I fell, face down and filthy, and by the time I scrambled up again he was gone.

First thing dawn, my head hurting, I went to Ambrose in his little room by the door, Ambrose who sat on his cot and listened, scratching his chest, and "You were drunk, young man, that's all. Drink does that to a person, helps them see what is not. Like Geraldina and her belladonna—"

"No. I mean, yes, I drank gin with Master Konstantin, but I know what I saw." Ambrose did not say more, but I knew he did not credit me. Who would? Master Konstantin? He would laugh, *Oh the drunken farmboy saw a goat, no surprises there.* No use to tell Geraldina or the others, to tell Annelise—

—who I saw that very evening, before the show, in the courtyard beside the goat-man, as he filled his little bucket at the pump. They spoke, or at least she spoke to him, what did she say? with her hand on his arm and her head to one side, like a cunning bird, a bird flirting for crumbs; so when she had gone I went out to where he sat, cross-legged before his cart; he wore boots, stout workingman's boots, but that did not fool me.

"I saw you," I said. "I know what you are. You should go away, quickly, before I tell Master Konstantin." He did not answer me. "You don't belong here, in the City."

"Nor do you." His voice was serious but his eyes were laughing,

laughing at me. "You are not from the City either. You are a creature of the fields, just like the beasts."

"I—I am civilized! I work here!"

"I work everywhere," and he laughed as I walked away, back into the theatre, what could I do? when no one would believe me? and all the players liked him, Suzette and Geraldina, silly Alma sitting on his lap, giggling as he pretended to feed her like a baby, chocolate smeared on her face but everyone thought it was funny, even Master Konstantin laughed. Even Annelise laughed, then smiled at me when "That drummer," I said to her, quiet in her ear. "That man is not good."

"What man is?" but she was smiling still, teasing me. She wore her spangled costume, the ribbons trailing black down her back, her pink skin flushed with sweat; I could smell her, a sweet clean secret smell. "He is a traveler," she said softly, as if to herself. "He has been everywhere, St. Petersburg, everywhere, every city in the world."

"Did he tell you that? Out by the pump?"

Her smile changed. "How do you know I spoke to him? Do you watch me, Sonny? Are you like those men in the theatre, do you like to watch?" and she left me there in the hallway, her smell still in the air, like something I could almost touch.

And I went out to the courtyard, to watch some more: for what? his empty cart? which was all I saw, there in the moonlight, the three-wheeled cart like a broken promise. Ambrose found me there asleep in the morning when "Get up," he said to me, not unkindly. "Move that cart into the shed, Pyotr will stay with us awhile."

"Stay? Why?"

"Ask Konstantin," but when I went to him Master Konstantin arched his eyebrows: "We can always use a musician, hmm? And the girls like him."

"He stinks like the mating barn."

"That must be why," and Master Konstantin smiled, but grew curt when I kept talking, tried how I could to say what I knew but "How is it your affair?" if the old man, old goat, old Pyotr made music for the ladies, tooting his stupid flute, the music made the girls wilder, which made the men throw more tokens, which meant more coins to count at the end of the evening, so "What ails you, Sonny Boy?" Master Konstantin said, drinking gin; this time he did not offer me any. "Shall I pull you off the door, send you back to the slops? Or all the way back to your greasy little village? Don't ask me about Pyotr again."

What could I do, *senhor*? as the days turned into weeks, as the spring came on, the time of power for things like him. I kept watch as best I could, trying to find proof of what I knew: as he played his music, the creeping, tooting, dirty noise of his flute; as he ate like the beast he was, that red mouth dripping spit, once I threw down a handful of straw before him to see if he would gobble it up, but he only laughed at me.

And I watched as one by one the players crossed the courtyard in secret, Alma and Suzette and Geraldina, it was no secret what they did there, all of them. All of them. Even Annelise. Watching her walk back to her room, wobbling like a foal, I cried, *senhor*, I know it is not manly but I cried. Because I had so much wanted—I had thought that perhaps one day, if I was civilized enough, I might go to her, Annelise, and we, she and I—

—but *him*, Pyotr, rutting there in the cobbles and the mud—and he was *old*, grizzled and dirty and old, and so I went to Geraldina instead, Geraldina who laughed but was not surprised, who did not say no to me; Geraldina never said no. Afterwards she asked, "But how will you pay me, Sonny? It can't be free, even for you."

"I'll give you something," I said, something for us all, because something must be done, and quickly. Because now Pyotr was wearing a player's hat, with golden braid, he was sleeping inside, under the stairs, boots on always but I did not need to see again, I knew what he was. And he would end by making beasts of us all, Annelise, everyone. Even me.

But *senhor*, truly, I gave him one last chance. As God is my witness, I went to him where he sat beneath the stairs, wrapped in a stable blanket, still wearing the braided hat, and "Go away," I said to him, through my teeth. "Go away from here now, tonight."

"From *her*, don't you mean?" but he did not laugh, only crinkled up his eyes at me and "Your name, your true name, is not Sonny, is it? What did they call you, back on your farm?"

"Yours is not Pyotr. Is it."

"Wise child," and he did laugh then, showing me his ground-down teeth, nubs in the jaw, and "Tonight," I said. "I won't warn you again," and I left him there, to collect what I needed, to finish my evening tasks. Geraldina tried to stop me in the hallway but I put up my hand at her, to say *Wait, wait until after the show*—

—which that night was very wild, I had to close the curtains early; Ambrose and even Master Konstantin had to help me, yanking them shut on the backs of the gasping, grasping men, tokens spilling out of their pockets, the players fleeing: Alma got her ankle wrenched, Suzette was stripped almost bare—

—as the flute shrieked on, old Pyotr on the side of the stage staring over all our heads as if he saw something amusing out in the darkness, playing on and on as the men were herded out, cursing and pushing, as Master Konstantin came back wiping his brow, stood shouting at Pyotr which was what I needed, all I needed, to go and fetch the gin and the wine, and "When it begins to cost instead of pay," Master Konstantin said, "that is where I draw the line. You see Alma hobbling? She's finished for the week. And Geraldina will have a black eye, the stupid cow. —Ah, that's good," as he took the drink from me, his bottle of gin, and the little tin bucket, Pyotr's own bucket half-filled with wine that I took from the cask in the cellar, took and mixed and mingled and "None for you," Master Konstantin scowled at me, "you can't hold your liquor, go on," back to the doors to sit with Ambrose and to wait, wait until it was later, very late and they were all asleep, even him. Especially him, snoring like a bull under the stairs.

And then I did what I know how to do, what Dusan knows, from the mud and the shit and the farm: to make a he-goat a wether, a neuter, all you need is a knife. A sharp knife, and some wine mixed with belladonna, and the job is done. If you do it swiftly and well, there is not even very much blood . . . I know you say you took his boots from him, and that his feet were not hooves, his head had no horns, but I swear to you, *senhor*, and to the Lieutenant, too, I saw what I saw and I did what was right. And civilized, too, *senhor*, I was civilized. I buried what I took from him, and I made sure to place his flute inside his coat.

THE MARBLE LILY

Honored gentlemen and judges, judge for yourselves, *consider* for yourselves: all the wrong I did was clasp her hand. And for this I am separated from my useful work, and my dear family, and subject to a confinement more solitary and cold than that which this poor girl, this so-called "Désirée," or "Marble Lily of the Seine," lay for so long unnamed and unmourned.

Nor am I mourned. My wife steadfastly refuses to admit to the merits of my case; she has gone into seclusion in Cluny, at the home of her sister, Beatrice. Beatrice has never cared for me; from the very start she opposed our marriage because, she said, I had dreams above my station, I was irreligious, with "scientific ideas." Of course I am a student of science! It is what brought me here to Paris and the Morgue, to learn more of the great and secret marvels of the body, while employed to provide much humbler sanitary aid. My wife, were she able to listen with an open heart, would understand that what I have done was done in that hope of knowledge. All else—the hysteric crowds, the chants, the filthy accusations—oh! so filthy! The human mind, gentlemen and judges, is the greatest cesspool in the world—all of that denies the truth of what happened in this room.

Explain myself? Shall I not begin where the story itself begins, with water? The effects of water on the human body are quite wonderful and well-documented, from the wrinkling and swelling that is called "washerwoman's skin," to the gooseflesh we all experience from a dash of cold liquid—even the living feel so, the living are not so very different from the dead—to other, more grievous changes produced when a body floats for days, such as this girl's had.

I have seen many such cases, gentlemen and judges; though I am but a servant, I have—I had—the confidence and approbation of my superiors, who marveled at my facility with the bodies, and how I keep the viewing glass so clean. The greasy hands and fingers of the public—! They are ravenous, those crowds who come to view the mystery of death, it is well-known that hundreds of them pass through our doors in a single day, during the sensation of the "fillettes de Suresnes" there were ten thousand here in less than one week! I had situated those bodies on draped chairs, not the slabs, so that the viewers might be able to offer better aid in the sad case of the little drowned girls. I myself affixed the identity numbers to their tunics, and as I did so I said a prayer to the Virgin, whose tender heart is surely touched by the lost children, now gone home to Paradise . . . And Beatrice calls me irreligious!

Though I admit that prayer was not my first response when I saw this girl. Still garbed in her servant's apron, pulled from the river by a pair of fishermen and carried by them to the Morgue: a female, aged perhaps sixteen, with fair hair that, when loosed and dried from its sodden plaits, hung nearly to her hips, and the still, calm face of a marble Venus—it is what the crude fishermen called her, that and much more, and swore that they had done their utmost to revive her, though "revive" was not the word they used, those rogues!—who were bought cups of wine for their so-called heroics, their names were even printed in the newspapers . . . *Her* name, let it be noted in the records, is not "Désirée," any more than it is "the Water Lily of the Seine" or "The Marble Lily," as she came to be called once she was arrayed upon the slab; it is likely that her true name will never be discovered. So many people have passed before her, avid to gaze and remark, yet none of them could say with certainty who she was.

Yet the moment I laid eyes on her, I knew her.

I see by your expressions that this admission suggests to you something untoward, unwholesome as those fishermen were unwholesome, but may I remind you, with all deference, that my own superiors at the Morgue were always more than willing to rely upon my vision: *Ask François*, they all said. *François has an eye for the dead!* Is that not why they allowed me, a mere janitor, so often into their forensic examinations, why they allowed me to take notes—you have my notes, my copybook there on the table before you; may I read to you, read that "the case of Female Subject so-called Marble Lily was"—Yes. Yes of course. Only to demonstrate that it was science that drove me, to learn further the mechanism of death: Was she lost before or after she entered the water? Was the cause truly drowning, or was she the victim of an assailant, and her body thus introduced into the river to cover the foul crime? And how long had she been in its currents and deeps, for the normal rhythms of decomposition are disrupted when— My apologies, gentlemen and judges, I only seek to demonstrate that my interest in this young woman was entirely scientific, to begin.

But the more I looked upon that lovely, lifeless face, alone in the dawn peace before the crowds—for I am the first to enter in the mornings, I am here before the orange sellers on the avenue—the more I considered her, the more the spiritual dimension of her situation began to press upon me. One hears tales of the saints taken from their tombs still incorrupt; and to find a young woman who had been so sunk—her clothing bore the marks of it—yet remained untouched by the grosser mechanisms that must attend a death in the water . . . Even my wife was moved to remark, at first, that the girl might be "a sort of miracle."

Do you know what a miracle is, gentlemen and judges? It is a gift from God to the brain.

And it was my brain that I put to work; it was that silent, unravaged face, that furled bud of a girl arrested forever in her blossoming, that I circled, with my thoughts and my vision, though busy always about my daily tasks. Thus it was that in those earliest mornings, I sat beside her—on the workers' side of the glass, not the viewers', why should I not avail myself of this proximity, as I sought the proximate cause—not of her death; of *her*, the girl herself, this nameless slip of flesh and pale hair, alive in the fact of the question she posed: What is Life? when death takes the animation from a body, but leaves it still so beautiful, and, when closely inspected, seemingly ready to live again? Why did we not, with her, need employ any means of preservation? for she did not decay, she lay there day after day with her eyes closed and her lips parted, as if, watching closely, one might almost see her soft breast rise and fall once more with respiration; as if she only dreamed of death, in a sleep so complete as to mimic its depths.

And yet in another sense it was as if she had never been alive at all, for though her photographic likeness was in all the newspapers, from the penny broadsheets to the *Herald* and *The Metropolitan*, and bruited from the salons to the streets—they even heard the tale in Cluny; Beatrice saved all the sheets—even thus so *known*, she remained unknown: without name, family, employer willing to come forward and claim her, nor even themselves to be found. A reward, yes, was offered, and what a sad farce that spawned: the woman who claimed to be her twin, and the oldster from Lyon, that antique fraud—! It began to seem as if she had drifted down the river from someplace farther than the countryside, farther even than France, from a place one can visit only in faith or desire. As the fourth week passed into the fifth, some of those who came began to leave offerings in her honor—heaps of lilies, picture postcards of the Virgin, notes, packets of sweets—*those* brought the rats—praying aloud, imploring her succor and aid.

Meanwhile I continued to watch, though importuned with increasing agitation by my wife, who demanded to know why I stayed, each night it seemed later, there beside her slab with my notebook, watching—for what? I cannot say. Is a mystery named before it is deciphered? I only knew that a process was at work, and that my own diligence was essential; perhaps some witness was required to bring forth what was to come, humble and obscure though he may be? Were there not angels present at the tomb of the Resurrection, stationed there by Christ Himself? For perhaps kind hands were needed, to help Him pass back between this world and the next.

So I watched; I made my observations and my notes, I drew diagrams. And as for those curbside chants, and filthy accusations—that alone in the morgue I touched this girl improperly, impurely, made sport with her poor slim body, that they found me in positions that— oh, it is painful even to recount the slanders, one can understand my poor wife's anguish if not her flight! But me! Whose interest was so pure— When first Monsieur le Directeur questioned me, I laughed!

No, M le Directeur did not laugh.

No. When M le Directeur heard the rumors, heard the orange sellers making sport of me outside our very doors, he summoned me into his office, and *François,* he said, *you have been at the Morgue for nearly six years now, is that so?*

It is so, sir, I said.

And your superiors say your eye is a keen one, that you notice details that others miss. Is that not so?

It is so, sir.

What do you make, then, of this "Marble Lily"? So I showed my copybook, that very copybook upon the table, and told all that I had seen in the watches of the night, I even shared my speculations that something miraculous was at work. I withheld nothing from M le Directeur! He is himself a man of science, I felt sure that he would believe and understand.

But it was he who instructed me that, for the good of the institution, for the reputation of the institution, I must no longer *stare and hover about this girl, what more can be gained by that? You see it is becoming a scandal. Do you wish the Morgue to be tainted by scandal?*

Of course I did not. Of course I do not! But—Yes, I disobeyed him. That is true, and I accept all blame and punishment. But when M le Directeur told me, then, that there would be no more public viewing, nor any viewing at all; that there was to be an autopsy, that that butcher Dr Grenouille was to take the girl apart, piece by piece, as a clumsy child might break a watch, to learn its mechanism—in my heart I saw her secret processes soiled, I saw her holiness destroyed, I was in such a state that I confess I did not know what to do, gentlemen and judges! To disobey one's superior is a very serious matter. But the girl and her mystery still unborn, what other friend had she in this place but me?

Before I did what I knew I must, I did the only wrong to which I may confess: I took her hand, that cold curl of palm and fingers, and clasped it as a brother might, or—as if we were both young together, in some strange Eden, light and fragrant as the Morgue is dim with odors—as a friend, I clasped her hand and promised her my aid. And despite what the penny papers may say, that is all that I touched, and all that I did.

The rest was easy.

I have—I had—access to the bundler and the dead carts, I know every hallway and corner of this great Morgue, and I know, gentlemen and judges, that now the girl, "the Marble Lily," named at last by me as the true daughter of Death, will never be found. For that, gentlemen and judges, *that* is the fact that came to birth, that is the secret that flowered for me alone, a momentous and dreadful fact whose contemplation brought me—through my vision, yes, that misses nothing, François has an eye for the dead—to a place beyond all dread, a place where death is as plain and good and necessary as flowing water, nothing to be marveled at, nothing to be feared: and she herself its emblem and ambassador, this girl whose body lay, as if on an altar, on the borderland, always dead, yet somehow still alive. She will stay so thus, she will stay that way forever, she is of both worlds and neither, and we meant to be her keepers and friends, and venerate her as one of the great mysteries given to us by God until such time as we will, by science, understand her pale unmoving animation, and use what we learn to help all who must suffer and die; which means all of mankind. If a miracle is a gift from God to the brain, then let the brain use it! Let the brain and the eyes—

Forgive me, gentlemen and judges, but what you say is as unfair as it is unkind. And may I state that whether or not my "eloquence is equal to my madness," I am not mad, the girl is Death's daughter, and until such time as you find it good to release me from my own morgue of death-in-life, that jail cell so dire even the rats refuse to enter, she will remain in the hiding place I chose for her, inviolate and clean, until God Himself calls her forth as he will call us all, to answer the Last Call—a day at which you, gentlemen and judges, may quail as fully as the rest of us. My wife and Beatrice, too.

And beyond that statement, gentlemen and judges, all I may say is that I ask of your mercy, the mercy of my copybook returned to me, and a pencil with a point that I may sharpen, for the lead I have now is beyond all earthly use.

• • •

[End testimony of François Undine, former janitor and servant of the Paris Morgue, found lifeless in his cell on 8 Mai 189–. The copybook was empty. Undine had never learned to read or write.]

LA REINE D'ENFER

Once, I said to Davey, *I saw the Devil plain.*

Go on, Davey said. *Save it for your fine gentleman.*

I did. A raven landed in the chimney pots, and looked straight at me, eyes all bloody red, and big as a dog, on my honor.

Honor's not in you, Pearlie.

Davey named me that, "Pearlie," for my fair hair and pale skin; the muvver used to say I was from the white side of the blanket. Davey had his own way of talking, and he taught me to talk as well, that is, the kind of elocution that gets a fellow somewheres in this world. The way the gentlemen like for you to talk, to pretend that what you do with them is a lark for both of you, a jolly wolly roly-poly while they're dosing you with the Remedy and sodding themselves off. *Do you relish the scent of juniper?* one of them asked me once, and I hadn't no idea what to say. Later I asked Davey, and he laughed: *Juniper is that gin smell, Pearlie. Allardyce's Remedy is just gin, with a little wormwood and a pinch of mercury for the clap.*

I loathe gin, I said, and Davey laughed again, for he was the one taught me what that meant: Not just hate it, he said, hate it with your belly and your teeth, that's *loathe.*

I loathe the Remedy, too, it works half as well as using nothing at all. Half the boys round here stink of it noon and night, and the girls, too, and half of *them* are fat as tadpoles, all swagged up with the next round of baby boys and girls. I am so perishing glad that I am not a girl . . . Davey says the only thing the girls have that we haven't is that a gentleman might grow so fishy-dotty that he will loop her to St. Paul's, which means to get matrimonial, and take her off the streets for good. Blinkers, that we call so because he's got a tic could blind you if you watch it too long, Blinkers says that where he used to Maryann it, up by Crispin's and the arboretum, was a corner girl so pretty and so fine that the second gentleman who had her wed her: *You should of seen her sausage curls,* says Blinkers, *all ribbons and such. And she could sing!*

Sing what?

Anything! It's how she met the gentleman. She was chirpin' at the arbo, by the gates outside, and the gentleman said "Why it must be a pretty bird." By this part in the story Blinkers would be blinking so quick-like it was hilarity to watch. Davey said that Blinkers must have been sweet on the little crimper himself, why he was so well versed in her whole story: *And what was it that she sang for the gentleman, Blinkers? Can you sing it for us now?*

Stop it, Paulo would say, Paulo the dark boy who sometimes plays that he is Italian or a Spaniard, even though his name's not Paulo any more than mine is Pearlie, he comes from Crippleton. *Stop it, it's not his fault that he—*

Saint Paulo, shut your hole. Go on, Blinkers, give us a song.

And then Blinkers would sing and we would laugh fit to split, always the same tune, "The Nightingale's Nest," tra-la-la, by the end he would be crying and Paulo would throw down his cap and say *See what you done? Why you got to be so bleeding dark-hearted?*

Shut your hole, Paulo. I knew that crimp, she had a jaw like a slopjar from suckin'. Anyway Pearlie can sing, too, can't you, Pearlie? which was not particular true but what I can do, and Davey taught me even better, is say verse. Just like one of them parrots the sailors bring home from India, say it to me once and I know it, and can give it back to you perfect anytime.

It was how Davey took me up, in the beginning, in the tavern where I was slinging pots, my muvver's friend's tavern though she was no friend to anyone and for certain not to me. Davey saw me, then heard me, then said me strings of nonsense, gammon and spinach, to test what I could do. Then he took me off and bought me a new pair of breeches and taught me the names of gentlemen, read them squinting off a paper he paid for from one of the hotel slaveys: *Mister P. Atherton, Esquire. Doctor Arthur Wells. Oh here's a one, here's a lord, Lord Kilmarry! John Adderley Walsington, Earl of Kilmarry. Got that, Pearlie?*

John Adderley Walsington, Earl of Kill Mary. Later I found out it was all the one word, but that's the beauty of it, you don't need to know what you're saying for the thing to work. And then he would take me round to places where those gents were known, and have me declaim, he'd call it, drop a name or two like I knew the gentleman truly personal. And in that way we would get things, lagers and such, or Trinidad tobacco, Davey was a regular fiend for the weed. Once I got a pair of fancy braces, the nicest things I have, silver-blue with a gilty kind of sewing up the sides; they are *flash,* those braces, I won't put them on against a soiled shirt. There was a hat went with them but Davey took it, which made me grim, since it was my declaiming that bought it and he has three hats already and I have naught but this old cap that I wouldn't use for a piss cup, all it's good for is keeping off the rain and not even that.

Why can't I have that topper? I asked Davey. *It goes lovely with the braces—*

Because I said so.

It's mine from the declaiming, ain't it?

And you're mine, Pearlie, so the hat's mine and your pretty face is mine and whatever you declaim is mine, too, got it? Got it?—smacking me all the while with the flat of his hand, and smiling, his choppers all brown . . . I thought I'd run away that night, hunkered beside the eaves at Freddy's alehouse, cursing him from under that stupid cap. Me who makes all the lucre, more than any of his others, me who gets him his fancies and tobacco! sitting there chastised, with my lips all swollen! I got no nibbles that night, the gentlemen don't like you so much if you're marred, unless it's them who does it—one time a gentleman wanted to burn me, put a hot pin to me in the shape of a Frenchy fleur-de-lys. I got myself away, but it was too near a thing. Which was why I went back to Davey: a fellow needs someone to keep the streets off, with the coin or the power or both, it's no good to be alone. But I was still that miffed that I said I couldn't declaim for the day, my mouth was still too sore—

Pearlie, now, don't be like that!

It's not me who made it so, is it?

—and took myself instead to the tea shop and then down to the panto, where they was putting on *The Crying Ape*, a fellow trussed up in feathers like an outlandish African chased by another fellow in a bear suit who was the Ape. The stage was that small that half the time the Ape chased the African and half the other way round, but they did it slick and got the crowd laughing. I kept myself to the shadows where I could scout the gentlemen, for it was my thinking that maybe I'd pick up a quick larker and buy myself a hat for secret spite.

But instead *he* picked *me,* that gentleman who said to call him Edmund: Mr. Edmund Chute, fresh of the countryside, of the school-room and the library and the books. I watched him come in and step all round the playing space, gazing and nodding at the curtains and the crowds, clapping for the African and Ape—until he saw me in the shadows, until I let him see me watching, too. And then it was closer, closer, closer still, but not like most gentlemen do, like I'm a sweet in a shop window or a piece of meat to chew, but as if he'd never seen the like of me before, which I could tell he hadn't. Mr. Edmund Chute, fresh of the countryside.

Finally he stepped into the shadows, he stepped right up to me and *Did that fierce Ape get after you, young fella?* he asked, joking-like but kindly too, like he would offer help if I should need it. *Or perhaps it was fighting? There are laws here against street brawling, you know.*

I put my head to one side, angled into the light to make my hair shine even whiter, like a halo; I sucked in my lower lip and smiled. Not a flash suit but a nice one, and he didn't smell of juniper, just Pears soap and coffee and clean sweat; his eyes were clear and brown as a spaniel's. I put my hand on his arm.

I don't bother so much, I said, *about the law.*

• • •

It was the first time I ever ate sauced quail, almost the whole bird!—and prawns in blue butter, and little rumcakes and quantities of boiled coffee, it gave me the headache so I had to chase it down with ruby port. *I'm glad the port pleases,* said Edmund Chute, *I'm not much for spirits myself. Coffee is my vice! "Black as the devil, hot as hell, pure as an angel, sweet as love." As the theatre is my mistress.*

Mistress? I looked around his rooms for a girl's duds or furbelows, I couldn't see what he meant. But he went on talking, to say he was a kind of teacher of the drama, who left his scholars and schoolhouse, his muvver and old da and younger sister—*It was a leap of faith, truly*—to come all the way to the City and put on plays, be what he felt called to be, what he called an *impresario;* I didn't know that word, but there was some Maryann in it for sure. He told me of his time in the City, what he'd seen, *all the magic of the theatre!*—by then he was in shirtsleeves, and braces not so nice as mine; it was late, Davey would be hopping when I got back, for missing another night's work. Be fucked to Davey. *I mean, you see, to court the muse, brew strong wine for strong hearts! We construct such a play now, myself and my company, about love, and terror, and damnation:* La Reine d'Enfer, *a beautiful lady makes her way to hell, to free her lyre-playing husband ... Did you know, Pearlie, that in Shakespeare's day, all the female parts were played by boys?*

If he's such a liar, I said, *maybe he belongs in Hell,* but I said it saucy so he could see it was meant for clowning. *Don't you want your play to tell the truth?*

He tried clowning back: *Why, I thought you said you didn't bother much about the law—?* But he swallowed hard when he said it, like Adam with the apple stuck in his throat. So I turned down the gas, all a-flicker like the panto, shadowy and pretty, and *I know some Shakespeare*, I said, and sat on the arm of his chair to give him the bit of Romeo and Juliet, my mouth right up against his ear. *Soft what light from yonder window breaks, it is the east'n Juliet is the sun.*

Arise, fair sun, he said; he touched my hair, his hand was trembling, just a little, just enough for me to see it. *And kill the envious moon . . . Pearlie, I should like to ask you something. Would you— Have you ever—*

O Romeo, I said, and tugged gently at his shirtfront. *Wherefore art thou Romeo.*

Pearlie, have you ever— Would you consider acting on the stage?

Spaniel eyes, the tremble in his hand—and food enough to feed an army, port and quail and prawns and who knows what else, in a cleaner room than Davey's, much cleaner, and almost as big as the one all us boys slept in; better than Davey's; much better than fucking Davey's. It's what we all want, us boys, to shut the door to the streets for good—and I would be the only one. Fishy-dotty . . . I sucked a little at my swollen lip; I gave him my very sweetest smile: *That's why for I studied elocution,* I said. The kind of elocution that gets a fellow somewheres in this world.

• • •

The first thing be bought me was a hat, a jaunty topper with a wide yellow ribbon band. I had to hide it from Davey for of course I had to go back to Davey's, until I could cut away clean, for Davey'd do the cutting, wouldn't he, if I was to drop him flat. Look what he did to Georgie Booters that time! And he looked at me particular strange, like a sniffing dog, he said, *What'd you get up to, last night, Pearlie? Where'd you go?*

Nowheres. And I'm here now, ain't I?

Don't be cute, and he hit me, but not in the face and not hard. That night he worked me himself, and I declaimed away, I sang all night like Blinkers' light-o'-love. Then he bought me a late supper at the Red Cock, sat drinking his lager and watching me, and *Pearlie*, he said finally. *You know I want what's best for you. Didn't I keep you from the constables, when you looted that doctor fellow and his packets of dope? Fine lad like you can rise in the world like anything, with the right help behind him.*

I know that, I said. I looked around the room, the dirty old Red Cock with its red walls and red-painted windows and smell of the Remedy; I almost laughed. *Rise like an angel. "Angels are bright still, though the brightest fell."*

What's that mean? In a squint, Davey looked just like a goblin, like the Devil's little bruvver. The red room, the scowl on his face. *Who taught you that?*

Dunno, I said. *I must have picked it up somewheres.*

You're acting different these days. I don't like it much.

Blinkers noticed, too—*You're awful jolly wolly, Pearlie, you must be gettin' some good coin*—and so did Paulo, who raised up his brows, and *Getting* something, *is our Pearlie*; he said it nasty. *Or someone. Does Davey know, Pearlie?*

Shut your hole, Paulo. Nothing's any different than it was.

You're growin' out your hair, ain't you.

Shut your hole or I'll shut it for you.

Fact is I *was* growing out my hair, for to play the Dark Queen, who was the Fair Queen now because it was me playing her. Edmund was all excitable about it: *I shouldn't dare to call myself a playwright, but to amend a character—And her name remains the same, Lady Frances.*

That's my name, I said. *Pearlie, it's just what Da—what people call me. My real given name is Francis.*

Francis, said Edmund; he touched my hair. *You've got the queen's beauty, certainly.* And then he blushed all over and hurried off up the aisle like a constable was on him. He hadn't touched me yet, though Davey would never have believed it, Davey who kept watching me like a puss at a fucking mouse hole, sending me places and then turning up there himself, to see did I show up, Davey who had me declaiming lists of names till I was sick of it, and all for what? A greasy meal, a pint box of tobacco, some stupid scarf that smelled of a fellow's basket, why would I want that? though *It's real silk,* Davey scowled.

You keep it.

Watch your tone, Pearlie. Take the fucking scarf.

A line of crows crying on the rooftops, my lines running round in my head—"To the depths of deathless Hell I'll go / No matter how dark the way"—and it *was* dark, that theatre, no windows in the back and the gas there-and-gone, but what Edmund called rehearsals was jolly larky. Trussing up in the Queen's glad rags, painted crown atop my head, though *He ought to have a wig,* said the freckled lady who did the dressing, but *It would be a shame,* Edmund said, *to cover up that hair . . . Give the incantation again, Francis, a little louder this time?* so *By all the spirits of the darkness,* I said, hands on my padded-up hips, *I bind you to my bidding, I adjure you to set my lord free!* declaiming out to the empty theatre that, the playing folk told me, was never so empty, for *There are watchers out there always, you know, ghosts that no one can see. Some are only watchers, but others—*

Especially with a show like this one! said the dressing lady, and she shivered; I thought she was having me on, but they were all serious-like: *Mind that extra devil that came to* Doctor Faustus—*thirteen up onstage, when there ought only have been twelve! I'd not stay here alone at night, not while this show's in play.*

I'm not afraid of devils, I said. *No matter how many there are.* That day I was feeling extra larky, for Edmund had been watching me like the king watched the queen, all longing-like from his prison bench: today Edmund *was* the king, as the fellow who played him—the African fellow, from the Ape show—was off somewheres or ill. So *Set my lord free!* I called out into that darkness, picturing the seats all stuffed with devils, crunching peanuts and flicking their tails, poking one another in the arse with their pointy rods—but it was

true you could see something if you squinted, like the air above the
seats was dirty, somehow. Like smoke, but not. Like a fancy but not.
*Deliver him into my keeping, you host of the lost, for I have spells
to crack your evil souls like lice!* And I put my hand on Edmund's
shoulder, and looked into his face all creamy, like the Queen would;
he looked back at me, and looked, and had to be reminded of his
line by the fellow playing the head devil onstage: *Hsst, Mr. Chute!*
"It is you I have awaited, my beloved."

It is you, said Edmund Chute, *I have awaited. My beloved.*

After the rehearsal, he bade me stay behind till everyone had
gone. Spaniel eyes, and clean sweat, and a bigger basket then you'd
think just by looking; and no Remedy, for I had no worries of the
clap neither, whatever he done before wasn't much. Afterward he
held my hands, he kissed my hands, and *I did not mean to do so,* he
said, *but you—Are so lovely. So very lovely.*

Come live with me and be my love, I said. *That's Shakespeare, too.*

No, it isn't, he said, and kissed me again. *It's Marlowe . . . Oh
Francis, live here with me, and be—my star, my shining actor, my
Queen of the stage! Surely the muses brought us together for that very
reason! And surely whomever—shelters you now will understand?*

Shelter? I didn't laugh, but I felt the laugh in my mouth, like when
you want to spit the spendings but you can't. *It ain't—it's not like
that. It's more like Davey bought and paid for me, except he never
paid, just took me—* And I made a story of it, a tearjerker cobbled up
from other boys' tales, Blinkers' sadness and Paulo's dead muvver
and my own muvver coughing herself empty though I made it to be
a sister instead and *Ever since she died,* I said, with my head on his
chest, *I been alone. I only went with Davey because I was afraid. But
now—*his heart started beating quicker; I could feel it under my cheek.
Now, with you, Edmund—Eddie— But he won't want to let me go.

I'll talk to him, he said. *One gentleman to another, I'll convince
him it's for your best.*

He's not a gentleman, Eddie. But I touched him while I said it,
in the way I was learning he liked, and he hugged me tight. I didn't

leave for Davey's till dawn was broaching, red across the rooftops, the theatre empty of its shadows or smoke or whatever it was, and no red-eyed crows to be seen. Why should I give a romping fuck for devils or the Devil or anything else of the darkness? Ain't I seen darkness enough, seen it all around me, Davey's brown teeth and that pot-slinging bitch at the tavern? And Blinkers blinking like sixty when I stepped over the threshold, whispering *Paulie, oh Paulie you better run*—until Davey put him back into the wall with one blow, then turned the buggy whip on me—

You traitor, after everything I done for you! Behind my back and taking trade, I'll beat the white right out of you, you lying little whore—

And he did. He did. Eyes rolling back in his head like a horse's, I screamed and tried to fight him but that made it worse, so finally I just put my face to the wall till Davey wore himself out, and left panting. Even Paulo looked scared, then. After some long time—it felt long—I got up on my feet, I wiped my face on the first thing I found, Davey's vest that he had took off for the beating, his quilted blue vest and I smeared it with blood, my blood, I spit more blood on the floor like a fat red flower. All the while Blinkers was sniveling—*Holy Mother, Paulie, Holy Mother, but he got you good*—until *Shut your hole*, I said, *on your holy mother*, for when did praying do good for anyone? What bright angels come to watch this show?

I grabbed up whatever I could put my hand to, a silver spoon from the table, a bottle of gin; then threw it all down again, my head aswim like being drunk. Then I took a steady breath and took up the things that were mine—precious little they was!—and rolled them up into a pillow bag.

Where you going? Paulo asked, quiet-like.

You're leaving us, Pearlie? Blinkers said. *But what should we say to Davey?*

Tell Davey I went to the Devil, I said. *And if he wants he can look for me there.*

• • •

It was the theatre I went to, the doors locked tight, but that made no never mind to me. I know how to do the in-and-out—and been caught at it more than once by the constables, not only that doctor fellow that Davey got me out of, but other places, too, and other lootings, and knifings, a boy's got to make his way . . . Eddie would want the constables for this surely, he would take one look at me and cry for the law. But the law knows what kind of boy I am, and that my name's not Pearlie nor Francis neither. Whatever law had charge of this case, my scalp torn and back welted and tooth cracked, a red line still running from my lip—I spat blood again, dark clot on the dark floor—none of it had to do with constables.

Out front, the banners said PREMIERING SOON! *He jests at scars that never felt a wound. To the depths of deathless Hell I'll go, no matter how dark the way. Set my lord free.* But when I spoke it come out twisted, my lips was twisted and the words all slurred, was it no Fair Queen for me, then, was that how it would be? May Davey and his fucking buggy whip be damned to hell . . . They leave a light burning back behind the stage, the dresser lady calls it the ghost light. In that little light the empty seats seemed more smoky and shadowed still, or maybe it was shadows in my eyes, both of them squinted with swelling, one of them half-blacked by the butt of the whip. I blinked, but the shadows hung the same, like clouds on a midsummer's day, you see them and you know the storm is coming. As I sat there bleeding, more words come to me, dark and quiet, like backwards poetry—*Propitiamus vos. Pandemonia. Consummatum est*—from another world, the world of plays, Eddie's world. The gentlemen don't like you so much if you're marred, would Eddie take a look and put me out, send me back to the fucking streets?

May God damn Davey down to hell!

—and this time I must of said it out loud, with all the hate that I was feeling, a mighty hate for the shadows come right toward me, just like a storm wind blows the thunderheads.

Red eyes, black birds, none of that is what you see, the bogeyman they call it, the hosts of the lost; naught like that at all. I think I laughed. Just like Davey, they don't give without taking, but I know how to reckon with that. I laughed, and said the poems, all of them—*consummatum est,* that's from church, ain't it? You don't need to know what you're saying for the thing to work—I *declaimed* the poems and watched the shadows boil. And when I finished, my blood was gone from the floor, just as neat as if some maid had swabbed it up.

I must of slept, then, for the next thing I knew was Eddie bustling in, jingling keys and whatnot, you could hear him before you could see him—and when he saw me in the seats he give a great cry and *Francis! What's— Oh dear Lord, what has happened! Who has done this to you?*

He took me to my feet and felt me up and down, then draped me on his shoulder like a baby; I think he cried. Fishy-dotty; I could have cried myself, I was so chuffed up with relief. It was me who finally patted his back, and *There there,* I said. *Don't, Eddie, don't take on so.*

But who—? Your poor sweet face—

His name is Davey, I said, and he kissed me, kissed the blood dried on my lips.

• • •

Cold compresses, and lots of ruby port, and a hurried-up rehearsal of others taking half my lines, Eddie insisting that *The rôle is his if he wishes, he is still our star* as the dresser lady rigged up a lacey veil for the crown, to hide the spot where my hair was wrenched out, and *'Twas a lover,* she said, *am I right? No one hits harder! Well, no matter, Mr. Chute will see to you. Now tilt your head for me, your ladyship, just like so—*

It will work out grand, I said to Eddie, though I was mumbling somewhat still. *We'll have our show just like we meant to. But first, we'll have Davey here.*

A brute who would do such a thing to you, to you, Francis? By

Heaven, no! We'll not risk such a thing, we'll have him in the dock instead, I'll involve my solicitor— But in the end he did as I wished like I knew he would, like I knew that fucking Davey would come with bells on when he got my message. It was Paulo I sent to bring it, Paulo I spied in the streets taking trade, and *You owe me,* I said, and he knew what I meant; was he ashamed, Saint Paulo? Was he the one Davey took around to the Red Cock, now? *You tell him to come at midnight, just himself alone.*

He's still perishing mad, Pearlie.

Just tell him, you sod, and he did, and *he* did, Davey, he came and came alone, into the shadows where he saw me sitting hoity-toity like a Queen. I kept my smile secret, I kept my hands where he could see them, empty like the seats around us, empty of what could be seen except for Eddie, waiting a row behind, all nervous-like and disbelieving. He had done what I said though he kept protesting to the last, almost till the clock struck—

But dear Francis—! It's not real, not magic, what we say; it's only a show. And this man is very dangerous.

I wriggled on his lap; I tugged his mustache. *But dear Eddie,* I said. *The magic of the theatre, strong wine for strong hearts! Ain't, aren't you an* impresario? *Don't you believe?*

Davey looked nothing dangerous, though he'd got a truncheon stuck sidewise in his belt and I knew where he kept his knife: he looked like a sad little man with a turnip nose, and a roll of fat at his gut, and wearing the hat that goes with the braces, he looked a proper fool. *That's your fine gentleman?* he called out, marching down the aisle, one hand wary on that truncheon. *Does he know, Mr. Schoolman, how many times you been dosed for the drippings? Does he know the law about sodding off youngsters, that could shut down a showplace like—well. None of that will signify, Pearlie, if you come home to where you belong.*

I belong here. I'm an actor now.

An actor! When he laughed it was too loud, like a bad performer too hot to show how funny something is. *I seen the placards outside,*

Mister Whatever-your-name-is, some farrago of demons and whatnot. Bogeys to scare little kids in the night—

It's not what you think, Davey. Once, I said, rising on my feet, *I saw the Devil plain.*

Go on. Save it for your fine gentleman.

I did. He was closer now, close enough for me to see the lager stains on his shirt, his crusty beard; and I marveled on how could I ever have done anything for him, ever been afraid. It was like if shadows were gone from my eyes. *A raven landed in the chimneypots, and looked straight at me, eyes all bloody red, and big as a dog, on my honor.* So close that we could have touched; I could hear Eddie breathing from behind me, quick as a cat.

Honor's not in you, Pearlie.

My name's not Pearlie. I could see his eyes, now. *I loathe you, Davey,* and I called the shadows in.

• • •

They said he jumped off the bridge into the filthy river, they said they found him floating at the docks; they said when they found him his eyes were gouged-out gone. They said a lot of things of Davey dead, but none of the things they said had me in 'em, for we was known to be fully on the outs, and me too broken-busted to do anything about it, and anyway I had a new protector, now; that's what they said. Davey's carcass went straight to Potter's Field and that was that, though Blinkers came by the theatre, cap in hand, to say hello and goodbye; he ended up with a broom in his hand instead, he's the one now sweeps the aisles and takes up your tickets when you come. Paulo I never saw again.

And the show, *La Reine,* went just cracking beautiful—a line-up every night, maybe partly from the gossip! And selling out on the matinees, we even got writ up in the papers: *"A shivering good show,"* the dresser lady—her name is Phyllis—read it out to us, backstage with our coffee and tea and port, *"wherein the good are rescued and the wicked punished, and the darkness vanquished by the light. Young Francis Chute is particularly affecting as the similarly-named Queen, as his uncle revives the great stage traditions of the Bard himself."*

No one made no comment on that "uncle," and I make sure always to call him so when anyone can hear or see, on the streets or in the theatre; though not in our room, the fine room with the fine bed, where poor Eddie is still having trouble sleeping, and nightmares too; he keeps on pondering whatever was it caused Davey to do as he done, run out the aisle like the Devil was after him but *Most likely his own bad deeds,* I tell Eddie, *especially the ones he did to me.* Eddie has bought me a splendid nightshirt, with buttons of real pearl; now I ruch it off and smooth down my hair, grown longer still, it is curling even on the ends. *They finally caught up to him and drove him right off his nut . . . Stop fretting. Come here.*

His conscience—true, it must have been eating at him. As we see in the Scottish play! And after that dreadful beating, he deserves no mercy at all. But oh, my conscience, Francis— *To have a man perish practically in our theatre, you can't think that it was the play that—*

Stop fretting. Let me be your conscience, though I don't give a red fillip; why should I? The nephew, the star, the light-o'-love, fishy-dotty forever or as long as my belly stays smooth and white and my hair stays pretty; there might be ways to work that, too, for the shadows play fair, blood for blood, better than Davey ever did. *Shall I make spirits fetch me what I please?*—that's from another show, that *Doctor Faustus* that Phyllis talked of, though Eddie says we shall not stage it, after what happened with Davey. So instead we're to do *Romeo and Juliet,* he the Montague and me the, what is it, Capulet. And after that maybe something comical, like that Ape show, and I could wear my braces and that cracking hat, I might could play here for a long, long time.

INSIDE

PAS DE DEUX

She liked them young, young men; princes. She liked them young when she could like them at all because by now, by this particular minute in time, she had had it with older men, clever men, men who always knew what to say, who smiled a certain kind of smile when she talked about passion, about the difference between hunger and love. The young ones didn't smile, or if they did it was with a touching puzzlement because they didn't quite see, weren't sure, didn't fully understand: knowing best what they did not know, that there was still so much to learn.

"Learn what?" Edward's voice from the cage of memory, deep voice, "what's left to learn?" Reaching for the bottle and the glass, pouring for himself. "And who'll do the teaching? You?" That smile like an insect's, like the blank button eyes of a doll made of metal, made from a weapon, born from a knife and see him there, pale sheets crushed careless at the foot of the bed, big canopied bed like a galleon inherited from his first wife—the sheets, too, custom-made sheets—all of it given them as a wedding present by his first wife's mother: Adele, her name was and he liked to say it, liked to pretend—was it pretense?—that he had fucked her, too, going from mother to daughter in a night, a suite of nights, spreading the seed past four spread legs, and prim Alice could never compare, said Edward, with the grand Adele, Adele the former ballet dancer, Adele who had been everywhere, lived in Paris and Hong Kong, written a biography of Balanchine, Adele who wore nothing but black from the day she turned twenty-one, and "I don't understand," he would say, head back, knee bent, his short fat cock like some half-eaten sausage, "what you think you can teach me, aren't you being just a little bit absurd?"

"We all have something to learn," she said, and he laughed, left the room to return with a book, *Balanchine & Me*: Balanchine in color on the cover, a wee black-and-white of Adele on the back. "Read this," putting the book into her hands. "Find out how much you don't know." Whiskey breath and settling back into bed, glass on his chest, big hairy chest like an animal's, he liked to lie naked with the windows open, lie there and look at her, and "Are you cold?" he would say, knowing she was freezing, that her muscles were cramping. "Do you feel a draft?"

No, she could have said, or yes or fuck you or a million other responses, but in the end she had made none of them, said nothing, got out. Left him there in his canopied bed and found her own place, her own space, living above her studio: dance studio, she had been away for a long time but now she was back and soon, another month or two, she would have enough money maybe to keep the heat on all the time, keep the lights on, keep going. Keep on going: that was her word now, her world, motion at any cost. She was too old to be a dancer? had been away too long, forgotten too much, lost the fascistic grace of the body in torment, the body as a tool of motion, of the will? No. As long as she had legs, arms, a back to bend or twist, as long as she could move she could dance.

Alone.

In the cold.

In the dark.

• • •

Sometimes when it got too dark even for her, she would leave, head off to the clubs where for the price of a beer she could dance all night to thrash or steelcore, a dance different from the work she did at the barre: jerked and slammed past exhaustion, hair stuck slick to her face, shirt stuck to her body, slapping water on her neck in the lavatory through the smoke and stink and back out with her head down, eyes closed, body fierce and martyred by the motion; incredible to watch, she knew it, people told her; men told her, following her as she stalked off the floor, leaning close to her stool at the bar and they said she was terrific, a terrific dancer; and closer, closer still, the question inevitable, itself a step in the dance: why was she dancing alone? "You need a partner," but of course that was not possible, not really because there was no one she wanted, no one who could do what she could do and so she would shrug, smile sometimes but mostly not, shrug and shake her head and "No," turning her face away. "No thanks."

Sometimes they bought her drinks, sometimes she drank them; sometimes, if they were young enough, kind enough, she would take them home, up past the studio to the flat with its half-strung blinds and rickety futon, unsquared piles of dance magazines, old toe shoes and bloody wraps, and she would fuck them, slowly or quickly, in silence or with little panting yelps or cries like a dog's, head back in the darkness and the blurred sound of the space heater like an engine running, running itself breathless and empty and dry. Afterwards she would lie beside them, up on one elbow and talk, tell them about dancing, about passion, about the difference between hunger and love, and there in the dark, the rising and falling of her voice processional as water, as music, lying there in the moist warmth created by their bodies they were moved—by her words, by her body—to create it anew, make the bridge between love and hunger: they were young, they could go all night. And then they would look up at her, and "You're beautiful," they said, they all said it. "You're so beautiful; can I call you?"

"Sure," she would say. "Sure, you can call me," leaning over them, breathing slowed, the sweat on her breasts drying to a thin prickle, and see their faces, watch them smile, see them dress—jeans and T-shirts, ripped vests and camouflage coats, bandanas on their heads, tiny little earrings in silver and gold—and watch them go and before they go give them the number, press it into their hands; the number of the cleaner's where she used to take Edward's suits but how was it cruel, she asked herself, told herself, how was it wrong not to offer what she did not have? Far worse to pretend, string them along when she knew that she had already given all she had to give, one night, her discourse, she never took the same one twice and there were always so many, so many clubs, so many bars in this city of bars and clubs, lights in the darkness, the bottle as cold as knowledge in her warm and slippery grasp.

Sometimes she walked home, from the bars and the clubs; it was nothing for her to walk ten, thirty, fifty blocks, no one ever bothered her, she always walked alone. Head down, hands at her sides like a felon, a movie criminal, just keep walking through darkness, four a.m. rain or the last fine scornful drift of snow, ice like cosmetics to powder her face, chill to gel the sweat in her hair, short hair, Edward said she looked like a lifer: "What were you in for?" as she stood ruffling her hair in the bathroom mirror, sifting out the loose snips, dead curls and his image sideways in the glass as if distorted, past focus, in flux. "You don't have the facial structure for a cut like that," one hand reaching to turn her face, aim it towards the light like a gun above; that smile, like an abdicated king's. "Once Alice cut her hair off, all her hair, to spite me; she denied it, said she only wanted a different look but I knew her, I knew that's what it was. Adele," the name as always honey in his mouth, "knew, too, and she cut off her hair to spite

Alice. Of course she looked terrific, really sexy and butch, but she had the face for it. Bone structure," almost kindly to her, patting her face with both hands, patty-cake, baby face, squeezing her cheeks in the mirror. "That's what you don't have."

And now this cold walk, each individual bone in her face aching, teeth aching, sound of the wind in her ears even when she was safe inside, door locked, space heater's orange drone and as late as it was, as cold as it was, she stripped down to leggings, bare feet, bare breasts and danced in the dark, sweating, panting, the stitch cruel in her side, in her throat, in her heart, tripped by unseen obstacles, one hip slamming hard into the barre, metallic thud of metal to flesh, flesh to metal like mating, like fucking, and she wished she had brought someone home with her, it would have been nice to fuck a warm boy in the dark, but she was alone and so she danced instead, spun and stumbled and hit the barre, hit the barre, hit the barre until she literally could not move, stood knees locked and panting, panting from fear of stasis as outside, past the yellowed shades, the sun at last began to rise.

· · ·

Adele's book lay where she had tossed it, square and silent on the bathroom floor but one night, back from dancing and sick to her stomach—the beer, something had not agreed with her—from the toilet she picked it up, skimmed through the chapters, the inset pictures and although it was very poorly written—as a writer Adele had apparently been a fine dancer—still there was something, one phrase arresting like a blow, a slap in the face: *For me*, said Adele, *Balanchine was a prince. You must find your own prince, you must make him your own.*

Find your prince: Prince Edward! and she laughed, pants rucked down around her ankles, thin yellow diarrhea, and she laughed and laughed but the phrase stayed with her, clung like the memory of motion to the bones, and she began to look, here and there, at the young men at the clubs, look and gauge and wonder and sometimes at night, pinned and breathing beneath them, talking of hunger and love, she would wonder what a prince was, how to see one: how one knew: was it something in the body, some burn, some vast unspeaking signal? The body does not lie: she knew this. And Adele—considering the small black-and-white picture, that arched avian nose, high bones to show like a taunt to life itself the skull inside the meat—more than likely had known it, too.

• • •

The body does not lie.

Ten years old on the way to ballet class, forced by her mother's instigation: "So you'll learn how to move, sweetie," her mother so small and fat and anxious, patting her daughter's cheeks, round cheeks, small bony chin like a misplaced fist. "So you'll be more comfortable with your body."

"But I am comfortable," sullen child's lie, head averted, temple pressed stubborn to the hot glass of the car window. "Anyway I'd rather play soccer, why can't I sign up for soccer?"

"Dance is better," the old car swung inexpertly into the strip mall parking lot, DANCE ACADEMY in stylized curlicue blue, cheap rice-paper blinds between MINDY'S DOG GROOMING and a discount hand tool outlet. Smaller inside than it seemed from the street, ferocious dry air-conditioned cold and three girls listless at the barre, two older than she, one much younger, all in cotton-candy colors; from past the walls the sounds of barking dogs. The woman at the desk asking, "Will this be for the full semester?" and her mother's diffidence, well we just wanted to try the introductory sessions, just let her try and see if she—

"I don't want to dance," her own voice, not loud but the girls looked up, all of them, starlings on a branch, prisoners in a cell. "I want to play soccer."

The woman's gaze; she did not bother to smile. "Oh no," she said. "No sports for you, you've got a dancer's body."

• • •

"Are you a dancer?" Shouted into her ear, that eager young voice. "I mean like professionally?"

"Yes," she said. "No."

"Can I buy you a drink? What're you drinking?" and it was one beer, then two, then six and they stopped on the way to her place, stopped and bought a bottle of V.O.—a princely gesture?— and sat in the dark doing shots as he undressed her, stripped like skin the moist drape of her T-shirt, her spartan white panties, her black cotton skirt, till she sat naked and drunk and shivering, her nipples hard, all the light gone from the room, and "The way you move," he said, kept saying, hushed voice of glimpsed marvels. "Wow. The way you move, I knew right away you were some kind of dancer, right, I mean like for a living. Are you in the ballet? Are you—"

"Here," she said, "here, I'll show you," and downstairs, hand in hand and naked in the dark, the lessening angle of his erection but he was young and it was easy, one or two or six little pulls and he was stiff as a board, as a barre, stiff and ready, and she danced for him first, danced around him, Salome without the veils: rubbing her breasts against his back, trapping his thighs with her own and since he was drunk it took longer but not so very long, not much time after all before they were lying there, warmth's illusion and panting into one another's mouths, and she told him the difference between love and hunger, between what is needed and what must be had, and "You're so beautiful," he said, slurred words and a smile of great simplicity, a deep and tender smile; it was doubtful he had heard anything she had said. His penis against her like a finger, the touch confiding: "So can I, can I call you?"

Dust, grains of dirt stuck to her skin, to the skin of her face against the floor. No prince: or not for her: her body said so. "Sure," she said. "Sure, you can call me."

When he had gone she went back upstairs, took up Adele's book, and began again to read it page by page.

• • •

No more ballet classes, dancer's body or no she was out and now it was too late for tap or modern dance, too late for soccer, and so she spent the summer with her father, dragging up and down the four flights of his walk-up, silent and staring at the TV: "Why don't you go out?" Lighting up a menthol cigarette, he smoked three and a half packs a day; by the time she was eighteen he would be dead. "Meet some kids or something."

"There aren't any kids in this building," she said. A musical on TV, the Arts in America channel; two women singing about travel and trains. "And it's too hot to go out." The air conditioner worked but not well; endless the scent of mildew and smoke, of her father's aftershave when he dressed to go out: "Keep the door locked," as he left, to whom would she open it anyway? Sitting up by the TV, chin in hand in the constant draft, the sound of traffic outside. In September he sent her back to her mother, back to school; she never went to a dance class again.

• • •

"It's a part-time position," the woman said. She might have been twenty, very dark skin, very dark eyes; severe, like a young Martha Graham. "The students—we have a full class load now—"

"How many?"

"Fifty."

Fifty dancers, all much younger than she, all fierce, committed, ambitious. Toe shoes and a shower, the smell of hand cream, the smell of warm bodies: glossy floors and mirrors, mirrors everywhere, the harder gloss of the barre and no, a voice like Adele's in her head, you cannot do this: "No," she said, rising, pushing out of the chair so it almost tipped, so she almost fell. "No, I can't, I can't teach a class right now."

"It's not a teaching position," sternly, "it's an assistant's—"

Keep the shower room clean, keep the records, help them warm up, watch them dance, no, oh no. "Oh no," as she walked home, hands at her sides, what were you in for? Life: a lifer. Edward's number was still in her book, still written in black ink. She could not keep both the studio and the flat: the futon, the dance magazines, her unconnected telephone all moved downstairs, shoved in a corner, away from the barre. Sometimes the toilet didn't flush. The young men never seemed to mind.

Adele's book lay beneath her pillow, Balanchine's face turned down like an unwanted jack, prince of hearts, king of staves: and upturned black-and-white Adele, pinched nose and constant stare, our lady of perpetual motion.

• • •

"You look awful," Edward said, stern as the young woman had been, there behind her desk: there in the restaurant, staring at her. "Did you know that? Completely haggard."

"Money," she said. "I need to borrow some money."

"You're in no position to pay it back."

"No," she said. "I'm not. Not now. But when I—"

"You must be crazy," he said and ordered for them both, cream of leek-and-tarragon soup, some kind of fish. White wine. The server looked at her strangely; Adele could be heard to laugh, a little laugh inhuman, clockwork wound the wrong way. "Where are you living now, in a dumpster?"

She would not say; she would not show him. He wanted to fuck, afterwards, after dinner but she wouldn't do that either, arms crossed and mute and "Where's all this from, anyway?" pushing back at the sheets, seemingly serene, not disappointed; his erection looked smaller somehow, fat but weak like a toothless snake, like a worm. The rooms were so warm, the bedroom as hot as a beating heart; the big bed still looked like a galleon, sheets and hangings cherry red, and "All this devotion," he said. "Suffering for your art. You never gave much of a shit about ballet, about dance when I knew you."

That's not true, but she didn't say it, how explain anything to him? and ballet of course brought up Adele: "You've never even read her book on Balanchine," scratching his testicles. "If you cared about dance at all, you would."

He was always a fool, advised Adele: *find your prince,* and "I need the money now," she said. "Tonight," and to her surprise he gave it to her, right then, in cash; how rich he must be, to give so much so casually. Putting it into her hands, closing her fingers around it, and "Now suck me," he said. Standing there naked, his cock begun at last to stir. "That's right, be a good girl, suck me off."

She said nothing.

"Or I'll take the money back."

The bills were warm, warm as the room around her, warm as his hand around her own and in one motion she brought their linked hands, his own hand topmost to rise, fast and sharp to smash under his chin, hit so hard his hand jerked open, her hand free, the bills falling to the floor and gone then, shoving out the door with her fingers stinging and burning, burning in the cold outside.

Adele was silent.

• • •

"Do you—" One of the young ones, crouched between her legs, her canted knees on the futon with its one wrinkled sheet, its coverlet faded to the color of sand. "Do you have condoms? Because I don't."

"No," she said. "I don't either."

His lower lip thrust out like a child defrauded, a pouting child. "Well then what're we going to do?"

"Dance," she said. "We can dance."

• • •

She got a job at a used bookstore, erratic schedule, the hours nobody wanted and every hour, every minute a chafe, an itch, unbearable to stand so still this way, medical textbooks and romance novels, celebrity bios and how-to books—once even *Balanchine & Me*, which she instantly stuffed into her backpack without thinking twice; why not? it was hers already and this a better copy, the photograph sharper, the pages not bent and soft and torn—taking money across the counter and she knew it was wrong, she knew it was not the right thing to do but sometimes she overcharged for the books, not much, a dollar here or there and pocketed the money, kept the change, what else could she do? The job paid nothing and took so much, stole time which she needed, had to have: no studio would hire her, no company until she was good enough, professional enough to teach, and she had missed so much, lost so much time: she had to make up, catch up, keep working, and there were only so many hours in the day, already she woke at six to dance before work, work all day and then out to the clubs at night for that other dancing that while exhausting somehow refreshed her, made her new again, ready to dance again so what else was there to do?

And sometimes—she did not like this either, but her world was full, now, of things she could not like—she let the young men buy things for her, breakfast, a bag of doughnuts, carryout coffee which she drank later, cold coffee in the cold, walking to work at the bookstore and then somehow they found out about the stealing, she never knew how but they did and they fired her, kept her last week's wages to pay for what she had taken and that night she danced as if she were dying, flailing arms and her head swinging in circles, she felt as if her neck would snap, wanted it to snap, break and let her head go flying to smash red and gray to silence against the wall: no prince for you, nothing, nothing from Adele even though she asked: what would you do? tell me, I need to know, I have to know what to do and afterwards, alone and panting by the bar from which she could not afford to buy a drink, approached not by one of the young men, no prince but someone else, an older man in black jeans and a jacket who told her she was one terrific dancer, really sexy, and if she was interested he had a proposition to make.

• • •

"Naked?"

"Private parties," he said. The smell of menthol cigarettes, a red leather couch above which hung a series of Nagel nudes and "They never touch you, never. That's not in the contract, I'm not paying you for that. They're not paying *me* for that." Gazing at her as if she were already naked. "You ever wear makeup? You could stand a little lipstick. Do something with your hair too, maybe."

"How much?" she asked, and he told her.

Silence.

"When?" she asked, and he told her that too.

• • •

Too-loud music, she brought her own, her own selection, twenty-two different choices from *The Stripper* to soft rock to thrash, she could dance to anything and it didn't matter as much as she had feared, being naked, not as bad as it might have been although at first it was terrible, the things they said, they were so different from the young men at the clubs, being naked must make the difference but after a while there was no difference after all, or perhaps she had forgotten how to listen, forgotten everything but the feel of the music and that had not changed, the music and the sweat and the muscles in her body, dancer's muscles, and she did four parties a night, six on a good night; one night she did ten but that was too much, she had almost fallen off the table, almost broken her arm on a chair's unpadded back and with that much work she had no time for herself, for the real dancing, alone at the barre, alone in the dark, and the winter, it seemed, would last forever, her hands were always frozen, broken windows in her studio and she covered them over with cardboard and duct tape, covered them over with shaking hands and her hands, she thought, were growing thinner or perhaps her fingers were longer, it was hard to tell, always so dark in here but she thought she might have lost some weight, a few pounds, five or ten, and at the parties they called her skinny, or scrawny, *get your scrawny ass movin', babe* or *hey where's your tits?* but she had gone past the point of listening, of caring; had discovered that she would never discover her prince in places like this, her partner, the one she had to have: *find your prince,* and although Adele made less sense these days, spoke less frequently, still she was the only one who understood: the new copy gone to rags like the old one, reading between the lines and while she talked very little about her own life—it was a biography of Balanchine after all—still some of her insights, her guesses and pains emerged and in the reading emerged anew: she's like me, she thought, reading certain passages again and again, she knows what it's like to need to dance, to push the need away and away like an importunate lover, like a prince, only to seek it again with broken hands and a broken body, seek it because it is the only thing you need: the difference between love and hunger: find your prince and find a partner, because no one can dance forever alone.

• • •

Different clubs now in this endless winter, places she had never been, streets she had once avoided but she could not go back to some of the old places, too many young men there whose faces she knew, whose bodies she knew, who could never be her prince and something told her to hurry: time tumbling and burning, time seeping away, and it was Adele's voice in her head, snatches of the book, passages mumbled by memory so often they took on the force of prayer, of chant, plainsong garbled by beating blood in the head as she danced, as she danced, as she danced: and the young men did not approach as often or with such enthusiasm although her dance was still superb, even better now than it had ever been; sometimes she caught them staring, walking off the floor and they would turn their heads, look away, did they think she had not seen? Eyes closed still she knew: the body does not lie but the ones who did speak, who did approach were different now, a fundamental change: "Hey," no smile, wary hand on the drink. "You with anybody?"

I am looking for a prince. "No," she would say, surface calm and back at her place—it was the one rule on which she insisted, she would not go to them—the rigor of vision, letting the body decide—

"You got a rubber?"

"No."

—and again and again the same report, no prince and no part-ner and indifferent she would slide away, sometimes they had not even finished, were still thrashing and gulping but these owned not even the promise of kindness and so were owed no kindness in return: indifferent she shoved them away, pushed them off and most grew angry, a few of them threatened to hit her, one or two of them did but in the end they cursed, they dressed, they left and she was left alone, pinprick lights through the cold cardboard, sweet uneasy smell from the space-heater coils: bending and flexing her feet and her fingers, all pared far past mere meat to show the stretch and grace of tendon, the uncompromising structure of the bone.

A weekend's worth of frat parties, at one place they threw beer on her, at another they jeered because she was so thin and would not let her dance, sent her away: it was happening more and more now, she might do two parties a night, one, sometimes there were no calls for her at all. In the office with the Nagel prints: "What are you, anorexic or something? I don't deal, you know, in freaks, I don't want that trade. You want to keep dancing, you better start eating."

What he did not understand, of course, what Adele understood superbly, was that the meat was not necessary, in fact became a mere impediment to motion: see how much more easily she turned, how firmly in command of space, of vertical distance—*ballon*, dancers called it, that aerial quality also called elevation—how wedded she was to motion when there was less of the body to carry? Why sacrifice that for the desire of fools?

"You must weigh 90 pounds."

She shrugged.

"Anyway you're lucky. There's a party next weekend, some kind of farewell party, the guy picked you out of the picture book. You especially he said he wants."

She shrugged again.

"He wants you early, maybe a little extra-special dance—no touching, he knows that, but it's like a present for the guest of honor, right? So be there by eight," handing her one of the go-to cards, an address and phone number.

Edward's address.

• • •

"Hey, I need a, I need a rubber or something. You got something?"

"No."

"Hey, you're—you're, like, bleeding down there, are you on the rag or something?"

No answer.

• • •

"You should have taken the money," Edward said, watching her walk in: the faux library, books unread, shelves full of silly crystal frogs, squat jade warriors, girls with ruby eyes. "You look even worse than you did the last time I saw you, even worse than that ugly Polaroid in the book . . . I can't imagine you're getting much business; are you? Is this your idea of professional dance?"

She shrugged.

"Given up on the ballet?" and pouring wine, one glass; then shrugging and pouring another, go on, help yourself. The hired help. Like a maid, or a delivery boy; a prostitute. "The man I spoke to said you don't have sex with your clients—is that true?"

"I dance," she said. The room looked exactly the same, same quality of light, same smells; in the bedroom, on the bed the sheets would be red, and slick, and soft. "I show up and I dance."

"Naked."

"In a G-string."

"'Air on a G String,'" sipping his wine. "Can you dance to that? Does it have a good beat? Christ," with real distaste as she removed her coat, "look at you. You need a doctor, you're nothing but bones."

"Is there a party?" she said. "Or did you make that up?"

"No, there's a party but it's not here, not tonight. Tonight you can dance for me; if you're good I'll even tip you . . . is tipping permitted? or is it added onto the bill?"

She said nothing. She was thinking of Adele, Adele here in these rooms, choosing the bed linens, choosing the bed on which, Edward boasted, the two of them had made love before the wedding, before he and daughter Alice were even formally engaged: the way her body moved, he had said, it was unbelievable, and "Tell me about Adele," she said, sting of wine on her lips, on the sores inside her mouth. Thread of blood in the pale wine. "When was the last time you saw her?"

"What does that have to do with anything?"

"Just tell me," she said.

It was here, he said, she was in town and we met for dinner, some Swedish restaurant, only four or five tables, best kept secret in town but of course she knew, she always knew about everything. "And after dinner we came back home," he said. "To our bed."

"How old was she then?"

"What difference can that possibly make?"

"How old was she?"

"You know, looking at you now it's hard to believe I ever touched you. I certainly wouldn't want to touch you now."

"How old was she?" and he told her, confirming what she had already known: like herself and the young men, the would-be princes, the parallel held true and there on one of the shelves—how had she missed it? a photograph of Adele, Adele at thirty maybe or maybe slightly older, that pinched stare relaxed now into the gaze of the true Medusa, queen of an older motion, sinuous and rapt, and "Finish your drink," Edward said; his voice came to her as if from far away, the way Adele had used to sound. "Finish your drink and you can go."

Shall I go? to the picture of Adele who without perceptibly moving her lips said no, *no you must not go, that is the one thing you must not do,* and bending, she took up the book, *Balanchine & Me,* from the bag where she kept the music, she had her own music tonight, Adele's humming voice in her head and "Take a look," she said to Edward, gaily, almost smiling, "take a look," and she began to strip, shoes and stockings, skirt and blouse, each piece shed deliberate as a blow, and "You're sick," Edward said; he did not want to look at her. "You're very sick, you ought to see a doctor."

"I don't need a doctor." Bra off, her flat breasts like airless pancakes, like starving people on TV and without music, without sound she began to dance: not the party dances, not even what she did alone with the barre but something different, more basic, closer to the heart of the bone, and as she danced—panting, sweat down her sides and her face, sweat in her mouth and Edward standing glass in hand, staring and staring and she talked about the prince, the prince and the partner and all her seeking, all her lost and wandering ways: was she talking out loud? and then to the picture, the photograph of Adele: does he know? can he learn, will he ever understand?

The body does not lie, said Adele. *But he is trapped in his body. He was always there, for me, for you but he is trapped, he needs to get out. I could not help him get out so now you must. Get him out—*

—and "Get out," he said: her whirling body, one leg high, high, even with her shoulder, look at those tendons, that flex and stretch! The difference between lead and air, meat and feathers, hunger and love, and "Listen now," she said: listen now and the little picture of Adele lit up, bloomed as if light rose from within, lit outward from the heart and with both hands she grabbed for the figurines, jade and crystal, frog and solider and threw them to the floor, at the walls, up and down to smash and glitter, topple and fall and, shouting, he grabbed for her, tried to take her hands, tried to join the dance but *he is trapped* and "I know," she said to Adele, the glowing picture, "oh I know," and when he came for her again she hit him as hard as she could with the ball of her foot, fierce and sure in the crotch to make him go down, fall, lie cramped and curled on the silence of the floor, curled about the red worm of his cock, the cradle of his balls: like a worm caught on the sidewalk, curling in panic in the absence of the earth.

The body does not lie, said Adele.

Edward gasping, a wet, weeping sound, and she kicked him again, harder this time, a slow deliberate kick: *En pointe,* she said with a smile to the picture, and with one finger hooked the G-string from the cresting pelvic arch.

ABOUT THE AUTHOR

Kathe Koja writes novels and short fiction, and creates and produces immersive fiction performances, both solo and with a rotating ensemble of artists. Her work crosses and combines genres, and her books have won awards, been multiply translated, and optioned for film and performance. She is based in Detroit and thinks globally. She can be found at kathekoja.com.